2047
THE UNIFIER

SOMETIMES HISTORY NEEDS TO BE REVISITED TO CREATE HISTORY

RASHMI TRIVEDI

First Published in December 2019

ISBN: 978-93-89763-74-4

BLUEROSE PUBLISHERS
www.bluerosepublishers.com
info@bluerosepublishers.com
+91 8882 898 898

Cover Design:
Mohd Arif

Typographic Design:
Tanya Raj Upadhyay

Editor:
Balakumar Ravichandran

Distributed by: BlueRose, Amazon, Flipkart, Shopclues

ACKNOWLEDGMENT

It's been nearly three years since my first book was published. Three years and three books later, I still feel as if I am living a dream. For a person not even remotely connected to literature and writing, to suddenly enter a new world, takes courage.

This courage is not always intrinsic; for me, it came with the support of the people from my inner circle.

I walked down the new path because I knew that they would catch me if I fell.

I knew that if I got tired and sat down to rest for a while, I would have the shade of their love and understanding.

I was sure that when the path got difficult and I lost hope, they would be there to cheer me up.

I was confident that if en route I lost my way, they would be the lighthouse which would steer me back.

I am thankful to the people in my inner circle, my family and close friends who are the pillars of my existence.

Every moment of my life, I am thankful to God for all the people in my inner circle. I am indebted to Him for giving me a blessed existence. When God has my back, I need not worry about anything!

When you are married for nearly a quarter century, you cease to become a couple! Yes, you read this right! You are no longer a couple because you become a single entity. My husband Viren, is a part of me without whom I cannot do anything in life.

I thank you, dear husband, for being the force behind everything I do. He also is my biggest fan and is very proud of whatever I do.

My parents with their constant love and support have always been my guiding star. Thank you Ma and Papa.

My son Eshan and daughter Eshita always give me constructive criticism which pushes me to bring out the best in me and my book.

My brother Mukesh and my sisters Poonam and Jyoti always encouraged me to write, and Poonam with her perfect grammar, often does the first layer of editing for whatever I write. I am so thankful to them.

All my friends, I don't need to name you, but you know that I am talking about you. Thank you, for your support and for being my friend!

I am so grateful to my publishers, team Hesten. When I first met Syed, I had no idea that the association would last for more than a few months. It has lasted for three years and growing with each passing day. We are both learning and growing together. Syed, did I ever tell you how lucky I am to have you in my life? Thank you!

Last but not the least I am deeply indebted to my readers for the immense love they bestowed on me. They not only loved my books and sent heart touching messages that sometimes brought tears to my eyes but they also kept on asking me as to when I would be coming out with the new book. This put me under pressure and resulted in the book which is in your hands now.

I now want to end with my magic mantra- Thank you Universe for manifesting all my dreams!

2030

CHANDNI CHOWK, NEW DELHI

She was lost! Lost in a strange country. A country not only strange but also hostile. She hated to admit this as she tried for the umpteenth time to restart her phone. But alas! It was completely out of charge.

She knew that she should not have ventured out alone this far, but she had wanted to visit Chandni Chowk. This was, after all, where her great grandparents had come from. She had always wanted to visit the house where they had lived. Of course, she had been foolish. She knew that now.

Her aunt, with whom she had come, had warned her against going anywhere alone. "Times are grave," she had said. "Wounds are raw and emotions are raging. So, it is better that a seventeen-year-old Pakistani girl does not go frolicking around the city," she had warned. But would she ever learn?

She had already boarded the metro by the time she came to know about some recent developments at the border. People were discussing about some firing along the LOC where, apparently, the beheaded bodies of some Indian soldiers had been found. Of course, all these were figments of imagination of the Indian media. Nevertheless, this was not a good start to her adventure.

She took the metro. The metro was for the masses—the lower class people, she had been told. She had wanted to feel like one and taste a slice of their life—be jostled in the metro, walk in the streets like a commoner. She had, of course, not planned for this contingency—out alone in the capital of an enemy country when nerves were raw, and her phone out of charge!

Damn! She did not remember even a single phone number. She could have easily hailed a cab if her phone was working. No cab was in the vicinity. She had no option but to do what she had wanted to avoid doing. The sun was sinking down the horizon as if it was in a tremendous hurry. She too should be hurrying back to be at the hotel on time, she thought, before her aunt came back to find that she was not getting pampered in the spa as advised, but was gallivanting up and down the streets of an enemy nation instead. She scanned the deserted street and noticed a small group of three boys. They were perhaps a few years younger than her.

She went up to them and asked, "My phone is out of charge. Can you please help me book a cab?"

"Sure," said the boy who seemed like their leader, for he looked very confident and sure of himself. "But why are you roaming alone today when the city is tense?" He seemed to be in a mood to lecture her.

"Where to?" He asked, as he looked at his phone to book a cab.

This was the moment she had dreaded. She took a deep breath and said, "Pakistan Embassy," looking straight into the eyes of the confident-looking boy.

The congenial face got contorted, and his face reflected a look of pure hatred.

"Are you a Paki? How dare you enter our country? You must be a spy. Yes, I had read that young girls are employed as spies who lure young men with their charm and then either try to brainwash them into betraying their motherland or kill them if unsuccessful," he said. All about booking a cab was forgotten.

He grabbed her hand and pulled her towards him.

"We will show you what a real Indian man is like," he said.

"Not 'man' but 'men'," laughed the other boy who had a very prominent scar on his right cheek. His scar, his laugh, and his leer sent a shudder down her spine.

She was scared now. She had read that the punishment for rape in India was death, but who would bother about a Pakistani girl who had got raped and murdered in India? In this era of high inflation, the cheapest thing was a human life!

"Look, I am not a spy. I am a simple Pakistani girl. I have come with my aunt who is a bureaucrat. I request you to please help me find a cab. I will be very grateful." She hated her pleading tone, but at this moment, her safety was more important than her self-respect.

As the confident-looking boy tried to pull her towards him, grabbing her roughly by her arm, help came from unexpected quarters.

He was the shortest of the three, perhaps also the youngest. One could make out from the sparse hair on his cheeks and upper lip that he was not old enough to have grown a proper moustache and beard.

He had a straight, sharp nose and thin lips, but it was his eyes that set him apart. She could see something in his eyes when he looked straight at 'Mr. Confident' and ordered, "Stop it!"

To her surprise, Mr. Confident did not seem very confident now. He grudgingly let go of her arm. He then looked at Mr. Eyes and said, "You, of all people, should not take her side. It's our chance to avenge your father."

"Will it turn back the clock and bring back the time that he has lost? Will it erase the scars that he is carrying on his body and in his heart? It won't. So, let her go," he said, as he looked at her tormentor with his penetrating eyes.

She looked at him again, and he looked at her. Their eyes met, briefly, for a moment—a moment that felt like an eternity. She understood why there was no resistance to what he said. His gaze was that of a man possessed. Without saying a word, it conveyed the message that he would not tolerate any nonsense.

He took the phone from her tormentor's hand and booked a cab. There was a very uncomfortable silence as they waited for the cab to arrive.

As she boarded the cab, she once again looked at him and said, "Thank you."

He just stared at her as the cab sped away.

'I should have taken her number or asked her to call me after she reached safely,' he thought.

'Oh, I should have taken his number and thanked him appropriately,' she thought as the dam burst and the tears, which she had been somehow controlling till this moment, started to flow.

2046

NEWHAM, LONDON

Fiza was bored. She grabbed the beautiful yellow satin cushion from her bed and threw it at Felicia. Felicia did not even flinch. She kept standing on the soft pink carpet near the dining table, staring straight at nothing.

The posh one-bedroom apartment, which had always been a source of pride for Fiza, today seemed claustrophobic to her. She pushed her chair away from the study-table, got up, and walked to the small book chest. These books were from her aunt's collection, who was still into reading physical books. She chose a book by a very famous Indian author, Siddharth Tiwari. It was a racy novel about an alien attack on Earth which she had started reading and was thoroughly enjoying. But today, it failed to hold her interest. She was so bored with her life that she felt like attacking someone.

The creases on the bed were evidence of her failed attempt at taking a nap. She had come back early from her work with the thought of catching up with her friends on the phone. Felicia served her coffee as she sat on her favorite rocking chair, calling up her friends. It seemed as if the universe was conspiring against her, since all her friends seemed to be busy at the same time.

As she glanced out of her tall window towards the park outside, she could see the London sky blushing crimson red as the sun slowly shied away behind the trees. She could see people strolling in the park. Many couples were sitting on the benches, some talking and some simply holding hands. She could see a few children playing as their mothers watched over them. Everyone seemed happy, except for her.

She suddenly felt very angry at life and screamed at Felicia instead, waiting for her to react.

'Calm down, Fiza!" Felicia said, shaking her head in disapproval. It made Fiza feel slightly better. At least there was someone who was not in awe of her and could admonish her whenever she behaved crazy. She felt like acting crazy now, and Felicia was the only person who could calm her.

"You should not let success get to your head, Fiza. You are not your achievements alone. You are also your failures. You are not just the awards that you have won. You are also the price that you paid for them. You are not only a corporate highflyer. You are also a person with needs and desires. Do something with your life, Fiza! Live it, don't just spend it…"

As always, Felicia's words had a calming effect on Fiza. This was the purpose. This was exactly what her mother would have said had she been alive. Fiza felt better now. Felicia was her attendant. This was working perfectly fine between them. Felicia was the perfect target for Fiza whenever she needed to let off steam, and she would not mind as she was actually a robot who was programmed to behave and respond in this very manner whenever Fiza screamed at her.

Lately, Fiza had been feeling a little lost and lonely. She had everything a girl could wish for: a degree from Harvard, a highly-paid corporate job in one of the best advertising agencies in London, a few very close friends, and a string of boyfriends who came and went. This was a big leap for a girl who was born to an illiterate mother and a father who was a good-for-nothing. Her parents were very poor; Fiza had lived with them till she was eight years old, when they had both died in a bus accident while travelling from Rawalpindi to Islamabad. Eight-year-old Fiza had survived. Her mother's family was well off, and she stayed with her maternal grandmother for a couple of years. Then, on her tenth birthday, she was adopted by a distant relative, a distant cousin of her mother. This lady, her aunt, whom she called *khala*, was a very well-to-do woman, with a coveted job in the Foreign Ministry in Islamabad. She was a divorcee. It was rumored in the family that her husband could not accept the fact that she was more successful than him, and so, had divorced her. Her proximity and closeness to a certain minister were also said to be another reason.

After her adoption, Fiza's life had changed dramatically. It was a typical 'rags-to-riches' story. She did her schooling from the best public school in Islamabad, and then went to London to pursue a degree in Economics. An MBA from Harvard was her dream, and she was elated when she was ranked the best in her batch. Her *khala* had come to attend her convocation. She was, by now, in a very senior position in the Ministry, and was often in the news. Success, which was denied to her in her personal life, was readily available in her professional life. Though she had adopted Fiza, she could never become her mother. Perhaps, she loved Fiza in her own way, but it was more like a duty. Fiza always missed having a mother to pamper her, to fight with her and to bear all her tantrums. Instead, she had *khala*, and a distance between them which she could never bridge.

Though *khala* did not approve of the way Fiza lived her life, she never said anything. But she preferred that Fiza stay abroad and come to Islamabad for short visits once in a while. Fiza too was happy with this arrangement. She hated politics and did not want to be a part of it. However, when in Islamabad, she would invariably get dragged into some political gatherings, meetings or parties. She simply abhorred all of that!

So, London was her home now, and she was happy here. She had turned thirty-three the previous month. Over the past few years, she had had a sinking feeling every time she cut her birthday cake. She had started feeling that time was running out. An underlying feeling of discontentment had started growing inside her. She somehow felt there was more to life than what she was doing.

In between boyfriends, there had been two serious relationships; one had lasted for two and a half years and the other for eleven months. In both cases, it was she who had called it off. She had had her last serious relationship when she was twenty-eight. After that, she had not allowed anyone to get very close to her. Fiza found relationships too suffocating. She valued her freedom and enjoyed being alone. That was, up until now. Things had started to change lately. She had started to feel lonely and aimless. It was as if she was on a journey, but neither the road nor the destination held any interest for her.

Fiza looked at the watch. It was 9 PM, and she suddenly craved for some company. At first, she thought of calling one of her boyfriends. Then, suddenly, she remembered that one of her clients was hosting a party and had sent an invite to her. They had organized a ghazal performance by a well-known Pakistani ghazal singer, Aftab Hassan.

Thinking of ghazals, she suddenly remembered Islamabad and her life there. Getting invitation passes to ghazal performances used to be one of the perks of *khala*'s job. For a moment, Fiza felt homesick. But why should she feel homesick? London was home now, she thought wryly.

She made up her mind to attend the party. Yes, she would not sit at home and shout at Felicia. She would go and attend the party and immerse herself in the music, she thought.

Fiza got up and pulled out a beautiful black dress from her wardrobe. She stood in front of the large mirror, contemplating whether or not to wear it. She put the black dress back into the wardrobe and took out the green *salwar kameez* which she had saved for Eid. She had bought it from the Indian boutique just three blocks away from her house. The owner, Alka, had become her friend, and she had talked her into buying this silk *salwar kameez*. Of course, she did not regret buying it, as it suited her flawless wheatish skin. The *dupatta* had multi-colored *phulkari* work, and after wearing it, Fiza would feel as if all the colors of the rainbow had come into her arms. 'This will cheer me up,' she thought as she started to get ready.

She slipped into the *kameez*, which fit her snugly and showed off her curves to her advantage. She would dress up today to look beautiful. She knew she was average-looking, but when she made an effort, she looked very attractive. Her long silken hair, which she usually kept tied with a band, measured up to her waist. She decided to keep it loose this evening. She then sprayed a light foundation on her face. She applied her favorite pink lip gloss on her full, sensual lips. After her hair, her lips were what people noticed in her face. They were just the right size, neither too big, nor too small. They were full, without Botox, and they were naturally pink, like the beautiful pink of a rose. Her nose was what spoiled the effect though. It was out of proportion with her face. *khala* had suggested surgery to get it corrected, but Fiza had never bothered about it. It's the personality that matters and not the looks, she felt. Her personality was such that men were drawn to her like moths are drawn to the flame.

Fiza wore her green contact lenses that matched her dress, and then applied green eyeliner. Just a hint of blush on her full cheeks, and that was all that she required. She examined herself critically in the mirror but could not find any fault. She was looking gorgeous, and she knew it; a whiff of her favorite perfume, and she was ready to go. She picked up her Jimmy Choo bag and felt ready to conquer the world.

Fiza entered the dimly lit banquet hall where the party had been organized. The program had started, and she glanced at the seating arrangement. The singer was sitting in the center and chairs were arranged in a semicircle around him. She noticed a vacant chair at the corner of the third row. She was conscious of the eyes that turned towards her as she moved gracefully towards the seat.

She stretched her legs in front of her as she tried to relax on the comfortable sofa. The ghazal that was being sung was a very old one and one of her favorite numbers. It had been written by the Pakistani poet, Fayyaz Hashmi. Many famous singers had sung it, but her favorite rendition was the one that had been sung by Farida Khanum, a great singer of yesteryear. Fiza closed her eyes as she let her body sink further into the softness of the cushion and immersed her senses into the music.

'*Aaj jaane ki zidd na karo, yun hi pehlu mein baithe raho*' – a lover beseeching her beloved not to leave but to be with her and sit by her side—such beautiful lyrics. Once again, Fiza felt she needed someone like this whom she could make demands to; someone whom she could love and someone who would love her back. It had been nearly six years since her last relationship. Even though she valued her freedom too much to risk it, these days, she was missing not having that special someone in her life.

Fiza's eyes were closed, but suddenly, she had a feeling that someone was watching her. She opened her eyes and looked up. She saw a man, probably her age, looking at her from behind his steel-rimmed glasses, which made her doubt if he had really been looking at her; but somehow, she felt that he had been doing just that.

He was sitting across from her in the first row. She smiled at him, but he did not smile back. 'Oh, what does he think of himself?' she thought, slightly annoyed. But then, immediately, she gave him the benefit of doubt. He was perhaps lost in his thoughts, or maybe he was staring at someone else in one of the front rows.

She shrugged and closed her eyes, to once again immerse herself in the ghazal.

Karan was in the royal ballroom of The Intercontinental, immersed in the soothing voice of the ghazal singer. When he looked around, he could not believe his eyes! The person whose thoughts he had been obsessed with throughout his growing years was right in front of him, just a few feet away. Of course, he could be wrong, his mind told him, but his heart knew otherwise. He strongly believed that if you really wished for something with all your heart, the universe will somehow conspire to bring it to you. 'This is what is happening right now,' he thought.

He kept staring at her. The ghazal singer was forgotten. The audience, the ballroom, and his friend, Riyaz, who was sitting next to him, were all forgotten. He could only see a young girl, spunk in her eyes laced with a twinge of fear, trying to look confident. Yet, the slight tremor in her voice and the fidgeting of her hands gave her away. He could see pearls of sweat shining on her wide forehead and the strands of hair defying the pressure of the pin and falling upon her face. He could see the beautiful face with big eyes and full lips, scared and defiant at the same time. He could see that beautiful face looking back at him with gratitude as the cab sped away. He still remembered the incident that had taken place sixteen years ago as if it had happened just yesterday.

He had just been a boy of fifteen then, but he remembered her face very clearly. Today, that very face was in front of him. He had no doubts about this. She had grown up into a smart-looking female. The long hair suited her, and all these years had only managed to make her look more confident and appealing.

Karan could never forget that lost Pakistani girl whom he had rescued from the clutches of his friends. God knows what would have happened if he had not been with them that day. That very morning, the images of beheaded Indian army soldiers were being aired on TV and printed in the newspapers. The truce had been broken by Pakistan, and the beheading of the soldiers was being taken as a confrontational action. Wounds from the war were still raw.

People wanted blood. People wanted revenge. People wanted war.

Only after calling the cab and seeing her off had Karan regretted not taking her number. He remembered that he had wanted to know if she had reached her destination safely. The city had been on high alert that day, and the situation around the Pakistan Embassy area had been highly volatile. He had often thought of her, and wished that he could somehow meet her to reassure himself that she was safe.

Every time he went to parties where people from Pakistan would be present, his eyes would irrationally keep searching for her face. Even today, when he had heard that a Pakistani ghazal singer would be performing, there was the tiniest ray of hope lurking in his heart that he might meet her here. Of course, one big reason for his coming here was his love for ghazals, and also the fact that his dear friend Riyaz had already bought the tickets for him. He couldn't thank his stars enough now!

Karan had always got what he wished for. Everything came easy to him in life. He never missed his mother, who had passed away when he was barely two. His aunt and uncle had brought him up. His father, who was in the army, was someone who only used to come on visits. Karan was in awe of his father, and his father doted on him. His father was a decorated war hero. In the Indo-Pak war of October 2028, he had been captured by the Pakistani army. He had undergone the highest degree of torture, which was humanly impossible to even comprehend. He had not only managed to escape, but had also managed to free his fellow soldiers who had been captured as well. During the process, he had lost a leg and an eye. He was proud of this loss and wore his physical handicaps as medals. Karan was very proud of his father.

Karan was a person who could do whatever he wanted. He knew he had it in him to achieve anything he wished for. The only problem was he did not know what he wanted in life.

During his college years, he had been very good at debates. The youth wings of political parties had approached him to join them. He had considered it for a while, but the thought of being true to an ideology never clicked with him. In fact, there was nothing he truly believed in. The moment he became focused on something, he would not budge an inch from there. But alas! It was rarely that he focused on anything.

His family and friends knew this, and they accepted whatever Karan said with conviction. The problem was that he did not hold much of an opinion about anything and would generally not insist on anything.

His father had wanted him to study accounts. So, Karan did that though, he liked political science better. But since he was not very passionate about political science either, it did not matter. His father and uncle decided that he should go to London to do his MBA, and he agreed. He was like a rudderless boat floating in whichever direction life took him.

Karan wanted to know this girl better. She had made a huge impact on him when they had met, albeit only for a few minutes. What a nerve the girl had! Roaming alone in a city where her nationality was sure to get her into major trouble. He had thought a lot about that girl those days, wishing he had taken her number. Today, his fantasy of meeting her was turning real.

He kept staring at her. Suddenly, as if pinched by the intensity of his gaze, she lifted her head and looked straight at him. He waited with bated breath for a flicker of recognition. There was none. Of course, it was stupid of him to think that she would recognize him. The incident had happened years ago, and he had just been an adolescent boy back then. Now he had grown a beard and wore large, steel-rimmed glasses. No one wore spectacles these days; they got the surgery done. But Karan was old-fashioned. He loved all old things. He still had an LED television set at home, while other people watched virtual TV. He still had his Apple watch, while other people used virtual watches. He still loved to travel by air, while the Hyperloop was becoming a rage.

Fiza looked at him and smiled. He was too dazed to respond, and before he could smile back, she shrugged and looked away. She then closed her eyes again and slid further down into her chair.

Karan knew what he had to do now. He waited for the interval when the singer would take a break and people would leave to get themselves drinks.

He slowly got up and went to the exit door nearest to her seat. Whether she went to the ladies' room or to the bar, she would be using this exit. He very smartly positioned himself there. He could keep an eye on her back from here.

After a short wait, a break was announced, and he kept his eyes focused on his target.

She stretched and looked ahead. Then she looked around. Was she looking for him? She stood up and gathered her *dupatta* around her. It was such a beautiful *dupatta*, filled with *phulkari* embroidery! Her aunt, who was from Punjab, had many such *dupattas*.

His target took out her phone and spoke to someone. Was she ordering a drink? Wouldn't she move around and socialize with the hosts, or at least use the ladies' room?

As if she could hear his thoughts, she got up and moved out of the seating area.

As he had expected, she walked towards the exit door. His heart beat faster. He took off his spectacles and put them in his pocket.

As she walked past him towards the door, he caught hold of her arm and asked, "Are you a Paki?" She stopped abruptly, taken aback at such an intrusion of her privacy.

"Yes, but who are you? I don't know you," she said. "I don't think we have ever met." She tried to remove his hand off her arm. He gently steered her through the crowd, holding on to her elbow as he said, "We have met before, but you don't remember me because it was years ago in Chandni Chowk in Delhi. The year was 2030. A Pakistani girl had lost her way and was almost molested."

He reached the bar and took a table for two. He indicated her to sit on the sofa. She stared at his face as the memory resurfaced. He could see her face turn a little ashen as she stared at him in utter shock and disbelief. The memory could not have been pleasant, he was sure.

"You are the young boy who helped me that day, aren't you?" she stated, not waiting for an affirmation.

"Of course you are! Those eyes! I could never forget your eyes. I had not thought that the young, sickly-looking boy would have so much authority over the other two tall and muscled ones! Oh! That is why you were staring at me!" She suddenly smiled.

This was the first time he had seen her smile, and it felt as if the sun had started shining in the room, and all the other lights looked dull and drab. 'Well, well! This is not the time to get poetic,' he chided himself.

"I never could thank you properly. By the time I realized that I had not taken your number, it was too late. But every time I recall that incident, I always thank you in my heart. I am so happy that I can now thank you personally, after so many years." She took his hand in hers and held it, her eyes never leaving his even for a moment.

"You can thank me properly once you sit down and have a sip of your drink," he smiled. She smiled back and sat on the sofa.

"Do you want to watch the rest of the show?" she asked suddenly.

"I love ghazal performances, but I think, right now, I am not in the right frame of mind to appreciate it properly," he replied.

"Why don't we skip it and take a stroll down the streets? I too am shaken," she replied, and seeing an affirmative look on his face, caught hold of his hand and pulled him out of the room.

This is exactly what she needed! Who could have imagined that an evening when she was getting bored to death, things could turn around like this?

She had felt those intense eyes much before she had seen him. How strange it is that women have the knack for sensing someone's stares! She was used to people staring at her, and so, it was nothing new. But what was new was that when she had smiled back at him, he had not smiled back. This had been so novel to her that it had piqued her interest. She had not looked at him again but had, throughout, been conscious of his gaze upon her. From the corner of her eyes, she had noticed him get up and go behind her seat. 'Oh, is he leaving?' she had wondered. 'Am I disappointed?' she had pondered again. Yes, perhaps. She had wanted to know why he had not smiled back at her. What did he think of himself, or more specifically, who was he?

That was the main reason she had got up and looked around during the break. Yes, there he was, near the exit door. She had decided to take the other exit, but then, at the last moment, had changed her mind and taken the exit near which he had been standing.

She had been taken aback when he had asked her if she was a Paki. The way he had asked the question had jolted a wire in her brain, and for a moment, she was transported to a place far away and a time far behind. She had managed to say yes, but her mind had been trying to access memories hidden in the layers of her mind.

When he told her that he had met her in Chandni Chowk, a picture of a young boy with penetrating eyes and an authoritative voice flashed across her mind. He had saved her from being molested for sure, and perhaps, rape and murder too. She had had nightmares from that incident for a long time, but in all her dreams, the timid-looking boy would somehow crop up to be her knight in shining armor, saving her at the last moment.

She had always regretted not thanking him enough. She remembered how he had not only saved her life but had also changed her attitude. Her faith in mankind had been strengthened. She would often think of him while wanting to share everything in her life with someone.

There was no one back home who she could share her feelings with. Due to the nature of her *khala*'s job, she was not allowed to mingle much with her friends and relatives. *khala*, though very kind and generous, had no time for her. It also seemed to Fiza that she had made a virtual protective wall around herself. She did not let anyone traverse her heart, not even her adopted daughter.

A stranger coming to her rescue and standing up against his friends for her had touched her. His act of compassion had lit a fire in her heart. Gradually though, the fire had died, and the memories had faded.

Looking at him after so many years, wrought havoc in her mind. He was certainly not like how she remembered him.

He was of an average build. The highlights of his face were the strong, pointed nose and the eyes now hidden behind the steel-rimmed glasses! Very few people wore spectacles these days, but he seemed to be old-fashioned, or perhaps he wore them because they suited him. The eyes behind the glasses were the ones she remembered all so clearly, eyes that had the power to make people do anything—compelling and penetrating eyes that could see through your soul!

So, God does listen to prayers! She had always prayed for an opportunity to meet him once in her lifetime, just to thank him properly. Her dream had come true. She felt like jumping with joy and dancing merrily, but this place was certainly too crowded for anything like that. On an impulse, she proposed leaving the *ghazal* performance and taking a walk.

The streets were brightly lit, and they started walking on the pavement. Just at the end of the road, there was a park which had fountains and decorated benches. As if he could read her mind, he suggested they go to that park.

"I still cannot believe that we have finally met, after all these years," she said, trying to let the feeling sink in, that the boy from her childhood, who had left a huge impact on her heart and mind, was actually walking next to her.

They entered the park and chose a pretty, pink bench to sit on. It was under a beautiful green tree that was decorated with small, colorful lights.

There she was, sitting with a stranger in the middle of the night in a deserted park! What could be more reckless than this? But strangely, he did not feel like a stranger. The hours she had spent thinking about him had somehow brought him very close to her. But the fact remained that she hardly knew anything about him. She did not even know his name!

"God! We don't even know each other's names. I am Fiza," she said with a smile.

"Nice to meet you, Fiza." He stood in front of her and bowed dramatically. "I am Karan. Karan from India. Chandni Chowk, to be precise," he said, with a naughty twinkle in his eyes. She laughed. "Glad to meet you, Karan."

As the breeze gently blew her hair on her face, her eyes sparkled under the lights of the park. Her face looked radiant and happy while he looked at her, enthralled, as happy as she was, perhaps, at this chance encounter. They both seemed to be in seventh heaven, happy that the secret wish that they both had nursed for so long had finally come true. They both had always wanted to meet each other, and finally, they had! Strange is the cycle of destiny and where destiny would take them from here, they had no clue!

They talked to each other for hours, sitting on that park bench. Neither of them wanted to break the spell they were under by mentioning anything about leaving. The morning sun was planning to make an entry into the scene, and the sky was turning crimson. The birds had started to chirp and announce that a new day was on its way.

It was Karan who mentioned that they should leave as it was already the wee hours of the morning. They hailed a cab. He first dropped her, and then he went to the pad where he lived. They exchanged numbers and promised to get in touch soon.

As soon as he reached his flat, he looked at the eye glass and the door opened. Riyaz came out of his room, shouting at the top of his voice, "Where were you? You left the program abruptly and you did not even take my calls!"

Karan jumped on the sofa and said with a big smile on his face, "Guess who I met today!"

"Who?" Riyaz asked, curiosity getting the better of his sleep.

"My childhood crush," Karan shouted, unable to control his volume in his excitement. At the same time, he saw a message flash on his phone. It was from her!

"It was lovely meeting you," the message read.

"Same here," he typed his reply in a frenzy.

"Dinner tomorrow?" he asked.

She sent a laughing emoji with a reply, "No, not dinner and not tomorrow. Coffee, next weekend."

"Done," he texted back with a smiley.

Riyaz was eagerly waiting for more information from his friend, but seeing that he was busy on the phone, he went back to his room to sleep.

Karan lay down on the bed and closed his eyes. Suddenly, he felt the urge to talk to his childhood friend, Vivek. Vivek was the friend who had been with him on the day he had met Fiza. He was the one who had caught hold of her hand. Vivek was impulsive and strong. He did nothing in half measures.

Karan called him up. Vivek picked his call after many rings. He was drowsy, and with half-closed eyes, he abused before even saying hello, "*Saale*, why are you calling at such an ungodly hour?"

"It's almost ten in the morning there. You better get your ass off the bed and do some work!" Karan grinned.

"Ok! Don't start a lecture. My parents do enough of that," Vivek said as he jumped off the bed. "Now tell me what was so important that you had to disturb my sleep."

"I met her, Vivek, the girl from Pakistan whom we had met in Chandni Chowk years ago" he said.

The expression on Vivek's face changed instantly, and he sat down on the chair to pay more attention to what Karan was saying.

"Oh my God! How strange! Where did you meet her? Did she remember you? Was she upset? Did you apologize on my behalf? What a fool I was to behave in that way!" He was ashamed of his behavior years ago.

"Relax! I'll tell you everything," Karan said as he narrated all that had happened the previous night, the night which changed his life forever.

Though Fiza tried sleeping, sleep eluded her. It was after a very long time that the thought of something, or rather, someone, had excited her. It was somewhat a surreal experience to meet a stranger who had occupied a lot of mental space in her growing up years. She had not wanted the meeting to end. In fact, she had barely noticed when dawn had started to break, and only when he pointed it out had she realized that they had been talking for hours.

She wanted to invite him to her apartment. She would have if she had found someone she wanted to have sex with. She did not. He was from the same part of the world as she, and despite all the modern advancements, people back home were still a bit conservative.

He was different. She felt different with him. It had nothing to do with physical attraction alone. He was attractive, no doubt about that. Even though he wasn't very tall, his features were sharp and he had an impressive face. It was something about his personality that was extremely attractive. They had been chatting like old friends, and he had not felt like a stranger at all.

Fiza wanted to share this incident with someone. She had only one close friend, and she was in Florida. Saira had been her classmate, and her mother was a famous singer. Saira understood the restrictions imposed on the family members of a public figure. Both she and Fiza had famous 'mothers' under whose shadows they had lived all their lives.

Saira had married Imtiyaz, who was a struggling actor, and their marriage was going through a lot of turbulence these days. Therefore, this was not the right time to talk to her. So, Fiza video-called her colleague and friend, Rhonda, who was the closest to her amongst all her colleagues. Fiza knew Rhonda would not mind being woken up at this early hour as she was an early riser.

She was right; Rhonda was on the yoga mat, doing yoga when she took the call. Fiza chuckled when she saw the image of her friend on the phone, upside down, doing *sirsasana*.

'Good Morning, sweetie. Up so early?" She asked.

"I am all ears, though inverted ones!" Rhonda said, as she came back to her normal position – the lotus posture. She was quite witty and humorous.

Fiza narrated the happenings of the previous night, and Rhonda listened attentively. After Fiza finished, Rhonda said, "It's the best piece of news you have given me, baby. You declare all the men boring and reject them. I must say that this man must be special, having held your interest not only through the entire evening, but right till the next morning."

"Rhonda, I am not so bad!" Fiza protested.

"Believe me, honey, you are worse." Rhonda made such a funny face that Fiza laughed.

"Grab him, sweetie; don't let him go. That is all I can say," she said, as she stepped into the shower and disconnected the call.

Fiza lay there on the bed, looking at the ceiling and wondering why she was feeling this way. Then she threw away the comforter and jumped out of the bed. 'I better go running,' she thought. Whenever her mind was restless, the best way to put it back to rest was to go out for a run, Fiza had figured out.

She grabbed her water bottle and stepped out of her flat to run on the jogging track of her residential complex.

After ages, Fiza was feeling excited about a man. She was looking forward to their dinner date that evening. He had called her twice after their first meeting and texted her daily. They met for coffee a couple of times, and the second time was even better than the first. They never ran out of topics to talk about, discuss or debate. After mulling over it for many days, Fiza was clear that she wanted to take this relationship further. She was ready.

She woke up fresh and reached for her vitamins. She was not in the mood for food. Then she asked Felicia for a cup of coffee.

Felicia brought a tray containing a mug of coffee and a few of her favorite muffins. Fiza smiled at her and thanked her. 'Thanking a robot?' She smiled to herself. 'But this is essential, otherwise we will forget our manners.'

Fiza took her cup and walked up to the window, which had an excellent view of the park. This was her favorite place in her apartment. She sat on the red leather couch, propping her legs up and resting her chin on her knees.

As she sipped her coffee, she looked out of the window at the park. Sometimes, the green trees reminded her of her own country. The national flag of her country was green in color. She did miss her country sometimes, but she hated the politics.

It was interesting that she was dating an Indian man. She had many Indian friends, but she had never dated anyone from India.

Pakistan and India were like two brothers who were at loggerheads with each other, after the division of their parental property. Both always felt that they had gotten a raw deal.

The country had been divided in 1947, almost a hundred years ago. A line had been drawn which had divided the country into two. It had not only divided the land, but also the souls. A lot of blood had been shed on both sides of the border. Many lives had been lost and families destroyed. It had been a nightmarish time, of which there were only bitter memories.

A lot of water had passed under the bridge since then. Many wars had been fought. Some government in-between had also taken initiatives and started a peace process – not once, but many times. But all the peace initiatives only ended with fireworks across the border.

The partition had created a deep wound in the hearts of the people. It is believed that with time, every wound ultimately heals. Surprisingly, this one never did. At the time of the partition, perhaps in the hurry to take control, all the loose ends had not been tied up properly. One major issue remained unresolved, and that was the Kashmir issue. It was not a big thing that could not have been settled with proper discussions, but the truth was that no political party on either side wanted a solution. They wanted the issue to remain alive for it helped them win elections! Enemy-bashing was a common pursuit in which both the sides indulged. They both claimed Kashmir was an integral part of their country, and neither wanted to budge even by an inch!

But unlike the politicians, the masses wanted peace. There was no doubt about that. The people who have lost their sons, brothers, husbands, and fathers in war can never be in favor of one. It is only people who have nothing to lose who cry for war and bloodshed.

There were forces across either side of the border that did not want peace.

Anyway, I will start my own peace effort at a personal level, Fiza smiled to herself.

Sleeping with the Enemy was an old English movie which she loved. She would be doing that, she smiled again as she put her coffee mug down and ordered Felicia to clear the tray.

She walked towards her wardrobe and wondered what she should wear. Technology had advanced so much, but still there was no robot that could tell a woman what to wear. Perhaps, they did not invent such a machine knowing that women would drive the poor machine bonkers by finding faults with all its suggestions.

After spending a great deal of time and thought on the matter, she decided on a hot pink top with a black mini skirt. She colored a few strands of her hair, the same hot pink. As the pink hair fell on her fair forehead, she decided to push back the rest of the hair with a clip and tie it with a pink band.

After the hairdo, she contemplated on the makeup. She was going out to seduce today. Not that any seduction would be required. But who can say, like Paki men, many Indian men are also old-fashioned.

When she was ready, she looked at herself in the mirror. Today, she was looking all chic and modern – a new age woman.

She picked up her Gucci bag, slipped into her Prada shoes, and felt ready to conquer India.

Fiza had booked a table at an Indian restaurant. The gymkhana at Mayfair was her favorite choice when she felt like having Indian food. She was a vegetarian, and there were better choices for a vegetarian in this beautiful Indian restaurant. It turned out that Karan too was a vegetarian, and so, it suited them both perfectly.

She had offered to pick him up from his flat, but he had said that he would meet her at the restaurant.

When she reached, he was already at the table. The ambience of this place always made her feel good. The name and design of the restaurant was inspired by colonial Indian gymkhana clubs where wealthy people socialized, dined and played sports. The dark red leather banquets, ceiling fans, glass wall lamps and wooden panels made one feel like a member of the nobility of yesteryear.

The moment he saw her, he stood up to greet her. Taking both her hands in his, he lightly brushed his lips against them.

God! When was the last time someone had kissed her like this on her hands? She could not remember.

On impulse, she went ahead and kissed him on his cheek. Karan loved the gesture, as was evident from his beaming expression.

His eyes gleamed like those of a child whose ardent wish had just been fulfilled. His excitement was contagious. She was already feeling high, and his cheerfulness only added to it.

"Karan, you are the first Indian man I am dating," she confessed.

"You are on to a good start then," Karan laughed. "You look lovely." There was sincerity in his eyes as the words left his mouth.

 "Do you believe in love at first sight?" He asked her very seriously.

Fiza was about to give a flippant reply, but the look in his eyes told her how serious he was.

"It has never happened with me," she replied honestly.

"Well, I think I am starting to believe in love at second sight. I have been thinking about you since the day we met again." Karan looked at her with his intense eyes.

Fiza felt as if she was floating on air. Her breath picked up pace as if trying to compete with her heartbeat. God! She was not a teenager anymore, and even during her teens, no one had made her feel like this. That too, without touching, only using eyes and words!

"I really do not know what to say. I know that you are special and that I want more than friendship from you. But let's take one step at a time. I am hungry. Shall we order food?" She tried to laugh to dispel the tension between them.

"Of course! How foolish I am to keep you hungry." Karan signaled to the waiter for the menu.

They ordered *samosa* and *papdi chaat* as starters along with tandoori potato.

She ordered red wine to go with it while he went for plain *lassi*. For the main course, they ordered veg *biryani*, *daal maharani* and *paneer makhni*.

As they waited for the food to arrive, she told him how her friend had told her not to let go of him. He winked at this and said that he hoped she would take her friend's advice.

They had met just a few weeks ago. Well, technically, they had met years ago, but they got to know each other only now. But, it felt as if they had known each other for ages.

Every time Fiza was with a date, her mind kept evaluating if he was worth her time and if he would be good in bed, and she would hope that he would not start calling her continuously after they slept together.

Today, she was cautious not to say or do anything that might turn him away from her. When the food arrived, Karan turned down the offer of the table attendant to serve the food. He himself served the food on her plate.

They made a toast to their friendship by raising their respective glasses of wine and *lassi*. Their eyes never left each other as they ate their food. They were oblivious to their surroundings and were totally immersed in the moment.

The food was delicious, but they were too distracted to notice that. They decided to skip dessert and leave early.

"Shall we go to my place?" She asked, looking directly into his eyes.

"Yes!" He nodded. His eyes had that glazed look, and he felt as if he was living a dream.

Was he really going to make love to the girl he used to dream about all his years growing up?

They left in her car as he had taken a cab to the restaurant. As the car navigated itself to her apartment, they held hands like teenagers.

It was Fiza who moved forward fast, and placing her left hand on the nape of his neck, tilted his face towards her lips. He was only too eager for the kiss. The kiss was like the first shower of rain on a parched land – tentative at first, and then becoming more urgent and intense.

The union of their lips sent wild tremors through her body, evoking sensations that she had never known she was capable of feeling. She wanted him like she had never wanted a man before. They started peeling the clothes off each other's body even before they entered the apartment. The apartment was dimly lit and soft instrumental music was playing.

They fell on the bed, wrapped in each other's arms. Their lovemaking was like a volcano erupting while their bodies burned in the heat.

After a while, they lay spent and exhausted. She enquired about the time, and Felicia replied that it was 3 AM.

Fiza did not want the night to end. She did not want the sun to rise. Unlike other times when she wished that her partner would leave immediately instead of waiting for morning, tonight, she wanted her partner to stay with her not only through the night but also throughout the next day, and many more days to come.

As their nations fought bitter wars, crying for each other's blood, Fiza and Karan lay wrapped in each other's arms, at peace with themselves, at peace with life.

There was no way they could have foreseen the storm that was brewing on the horizon, which would not only play havoc in their lives, but also change the fate of their two nations forever.

NEW DELHI

Anu was getting ready for work. She was running late today as the morning session of yoga had stretched far longer than usual. In the mornings, she taught yoga in a nearby park where people of all age groups, shapes, and sizes came for a walk and later joined her class.

Today, after the class, an old uncle had started enquiring about some *asanas* for his aching knee. Though she was getting late, she did not have the heart to say no to him and had started showing him the *asanas* that would be good for him.

After finishing, she kick-started her bike and rushed to her single-room flat in Saket. She entered the flat and straightaway went into the bathroom for a bath. It hardly took her five minutes, and she came out wrapped in a towel, drying her short hair with another towel. She hurriedly got into a pair of jeans and a loose *kurta*.

Without bothering to comb her hair, she hastily applied some moisturizer on her face, which was her only makeup. She had a plain but attractive face with deep-set eyes. Her nose was too big, and her lips were so shaped that she always seemed to be smiling. She smiled at herself in the mirror as she wore beautiful *jhumkas* and a matching set of bangles. These two accessories were her only indulgence.

She was running short on time, and so, she decided to skip breakfast. She grabbed an apple and took her '*jhola*' from the table. She never carried a handbag. She always carried her *jhola*, which she would sling across her shoulders.

Anu ran an NGO that worked for peace. She had founded it when she was only 21. She was 28 years old now. Her work was her passion, and it gave meaning to her life. As a small kid who had been born and brought up in Punjabi Bagh, she had heard many stories about how her great-grandfathers had migrated from Pakistan during the partition. Her uncle, who had been a soldier in the Indian Army, was martyred during the Indo-Pak war of 2028. She had only been ten years old then, but remembered how his mortal remains had been brought home wrapped in the tricolor. He had been her favorite uncle. He used to get her gifts every time he visited. He used to tell stories about his army life, which she found extremely fascinating and exciting.

Anu's aunty had been six months pregnant when he had died. To this day, she could never forget her soul-shattering scream when she had seen her husband's dead body.

That was the day she decided that she hated wars and they had to stop. She had no idea how she was going to do this, but one thing was clear—she would have to become powerful enough to bring any change in the society. Power and authority were what were required, and she intended to get them somehow. After graduating in Political Science with Honors from St. Stephens College, she enrolled in JNU for her masters. This is when she founded her NGO— Messengers of Peace.

During her tenure in the university, she had met many enlightened and intellectual people. Some were quite radical in their thinking, some highly conservative. This was a period when she had learnt a lot. She had absorbed everything like a sponge and later retained only what she thought would be useful to her.

After completing her masters from JNU, Anu completely immersed herself in her work. Through her good contacts, funds also started pouring in easily. A dream which she had dreamt alone was now employing eight full-time workers and about 5000 volunteers across the country. She was slowly but surely getting there!

Their job was to spread the message of peace — peace amongst neighbors, peace amongst different religions and peace across all borders. They would go to villages and communities to work with people who had been victims of any kind of violence. They would go to schools and colleges and try to garner volunteers from amongst the youngsters.

The youth today was sick of the violence in the world. Every other day there would be a bomb blast, taking lives, and later some terrorist group with some godforsaken agenda would claim the honor. It was frightening to think and imagine where society was heading.

The best time to talk to people was when they were open to change — during the time when they were in schools and colleges. That was when Anu tried to get their attention. Of course, online campaigns to get volunteers were always on. Her idea was that even if a single person got convinced about her idea of peace, the world would be a slightly better place.

A journey of a thousand miles begins with a small step. Anu's movement for peace was gathering momentum and was catching the imagination of people, especially the youth. She felt good that she was bringing in the change she had always wanted to see in the society ever since she was a child, but more than that, she knew that she was on her way to realizing her dreams!

With a smile on her lips and an apple in her hand, she skipped down the stairs to chase her dreams.

The alarm was ringing incessantly. Sooraj waved his hand and it stopped. He ducked his head inside the covers once again for another snooze. It was then that he remembered that he had to go for a job interview. He had cleared all the initial rounds and only the final interview was remaining. He was sure he wouldn't make it today as well. Nevertheless, he had to appear for the interview. He owed it to his mother who had raised him through a lot of struggle and hardships. She was a history teacher at Central School. Sooraj's father was an art teacher at the same school. They lived in a rented apartment near the school. Sooraj and his younger sister, Simi, were the apples of their parents' eyes.

It came as a shock for the family when the father became a victim of a bomb blast at the *Akshardham* temple. He had taken his students for a visit to the temple that day to show the beautiful murals and engravings on the temple walls. The group of two teachers and twenty students were at the spot where the bomb had exploded. None of them survived.

It was Sooraj's twelfth birthday, and he was waiting for his dad as he had promised to buy him a Google watch that day, something Sooraj had been wanting for a long time. It was a very expensive watch, much beyond the means of his parents, but his dad had promised to buy it for him and he always kept his promises.

The news of the bomb blast reached his mother before it was shown on TV. The driver of the bus was a witness and had contacted the school. The events in the aftermath of the blast had got permanently imprinted on young Sooraj's mind. He had accompanied his mother to the morgue to identify the remains of his father's body. They did not even get a proper body for burial. An arm and both the legs were missing.

A terrorist group from Pakistan claimed the credits for the blast. The city was placed under curfew, and it was in this tense situation that the cremation was held.

Twelve-year-old Sooraj bid goodbye to his childhood the day he lit his father's funeral pyre. He felt responsible for his mother and his younger sister, who was barely ten then.

Running the household with just one salary was difficult, but they managed. They vacated their rented apartment at Defence Colony and shifted to a much cheaper two-bedroom flat at Khanpur.

The death of his father had made Sooraj very bitter. On the internet, he met many people like him who had directly or indirectly been victims of Islamic terror. Without telling his mother, he joined a group called Hindu Maha Morcha. Their main aim was to consolidate the Hindu forces in the country and if required, take up arms to save the country from the pro-Pakistani Muslims and pseudo-liberals.

Though he had joined when he was 18, over the past ten years, Sooraj had become an active member of the group and had reached a level where he was very close to the top leaders.

Their party had also contested the elections and they had three members in the legislative assembly. They were all working very hard to get more seats for their party in the next elections.

The only problem was that Sooraj's mother did not approve of his political involvement. She wanted him to take up a regular job. He had completed his graduation in commerce and had done a management course from an online university.

At her behest, he applied for jobs, but in most of the places, once his political affiliations were known, he was rejected. He himself did not want the job, for he needed to devote more time to the party. His leaders had reposed a lot of faith in him, and he was also drawing a small stipend for the work he did. He did not have much needs and was thus, contended. It was only to please his mother that he appeared for these interviews.

The fire that had engulfed his father in its flames was still burning in his heart. If he would have had the power and the means, he would blow up entire Pakistan with a nuclear bomb. But he knew he could not. The only thing that he could do was help bring such people to power who would not bow down to global pressure and talk of peace with Pakistan. What was required now was one bold leader who would decide to wage war against them.

The war of 2028 was still fresh in his mind. Pakistan had attacked when India was reeling under the effects of an epidemic — the break of a biological disease in many parts of the country. The country was trying to save lives and control the outbreak of the disease. The war had lasted for nearly two months, after which Pakistan conceded defeat.

Even then, India did not teach Pakistan a proper lesson, but on the contrary, succumbed to the global pressure to settle the matter and end the war. If only he had the power, he would have definitely taught them a lesson!

If the political leadership of the country had been strong, they would have broken the backbone of Pakistan's economy before talking about ceasefire or peace. But they did not. Pakistan kept quiet only for six months and then resumed its cross-border terrorist activities.

Sooraj's dream was to bring his own people to power one day, and then he would be able to mete out the treatment that Pakistan really deserved. He would get that power in his grasp someday, and then the world would see.

With this desire burning in his heart like a fire, he got up from his bed and went to the kitchen to make himself some tea.

LONDON

Karan and Fiza were celebrating their half-yearly love anniversary. Karan had booked a table at the same restaurant where they had had their first date. This was going to be special because Karan had decided to propose to Fiza.

He had never thought about marriage even though his uncle had suggested it to him many times in the past. He did not feel like getting married. After meeting Fiza though, his outlook had changed. He wanted to spend every single minute with her. They would talk for hours on the phone, and after he decided to move in with her, the only time they were not together was when they were working. Even at work, they would be constantly in touch, texting each other. They just could not get enough of each other.

Surprisingly, Karan did not find this proximity stifling. He felt close to her like he had never felt close to anyone in his life, not even his closest friends. Perhaps, if he had a mother or a sister, he would be this close to them, but he had no means of knowing that.

He loved to cook for her whenever he had time. She simply loved the *peas pulao* he made. Once, he had surprised her with a complete Indian meal with rice, *dal, bhindi ki sabzi* and onion *raita*. He had bought *roti* and *gulab jamun* from the market. She liked it so much that she could not stop talking about it for days.

He knew that Fiza felt the same way about him. After knowing her past, he could relate to her better. Neither of them had had a normal childhood, and there was a vacuum in their hearts which no one had ever filled. Now, after meeting each other, they both felt complete.

He knew that she was not expecting his proposal and would be surprised by it. He hoped that she would say yes without pondering too much about the decision. The more one thinks about anything, the more difficult it becomes to take a call. Certain decisions should be taken by the heart and not by the mind.

He had bought her a beautiful emerald ring since green was her favorite color. There were small diamonds and garnets embedded around the emerald. In fact, the ring had all the colors of both their flags. It's funny how when you are away from family, you miss your family, and when you are away from your country, you miss your country. When you are with them, you don't really value either.

Karan had ordered a cake in the shape of India's and Pakistan's map, and in between, on the border, the ring would be strategically placed in a heart-shaped box. The cake had the words 'Can India and Pakistan be one again?' written on it in red icing. He had also hired a violinist to play her favorite yesteryear Hindi song, "*Kaun tujhe yun pyar karega*," from an old movie made on the life of a legendary ace cricketer of India.

They both entered the restaurant hand-in-hand. The attendant appeared promptly and pointed towards the table reserved for them. It was a table at the corner as Karan had specifically requested. The table cover was of bright red color, on which a small crystal vase stood glistening. The beautiful red rose peeping out from the vase was looking resplendent, just like a *bindi* on an Indian maiden's forehead. Karan gently guided Fiza by her elbow to their corner-side table. As Fiza sat down on the sofa, a violinist appeared from nowhere and started playing her favorite number. She was thrilled, and her face glowed with happiness. Just then, the waiter appeared with the cake. Karan motioned Fiza to close her eyes. She was baffled with the request but she complied. Karan signaled the waiter to keep the cake down on the table in front of her. As the waiter left the table, Karan asked her to open her eyes.

Fiza opened her eyes and looked at the cake in amazement. She was motionless, and Karan felt as if time had come to a standstill. He could not even breathe properly as he waited for her reaction.

As she looked up and into his eyes, Karan could hear his own heart thumping madly in his chest. With a steady gaze and stable voice, she gave an answer to the question on the cake, "I don't think India and Pakistan can ever be one nation again."

Karan felt his world crashing down as he looked at her, his eyes pleading her to continue. "But," she continued at the same time, coming over to his side of the table, "Nothing can stop us from becoming one," she said and gave him a big kiss.

Karan held her tight in his embrace, a little conscious at the same time to not end up suffocating her. The violinist continued to play more songs. Karan wished that all the clocks in the world would stop and this moment would continue forever. He felt as if he was floating in the air. It was the huge round of applause from the staff and the other guests which actually brought them back to earth.

"Karan, I didn't know you were so romantic!" Fiza said, her eyes sparkling like a diamond.

"You don't know many things about your Hindustani friend yet, and I will need a lifetime to tell you," Karan said as he pulled Fiza down on his side of the sofa.

They went on with their dinner, laughing and giggling at times. They talked while looking adoringly at each other as time just flew. They were like spectators on a beautiful bridge watching time pass underneath them like a flowing river, each moment shining like silver, painting a colorful story.

NEW DELHI

The weather was perfect in Delhi during this part of the year. There was a slight nip in the air as the year was changing seasons. By no stretch of the imagination could the weather be called warm, but looking at Raunak Thakur, one would think that it was a summer afternoon. Raunak was pacing up and down the room in his Chandni Chowk residence.

Raunak, a tall man in his sixties, stood wiping his forehead with a kerchief, and wore the facial expression of someone who had just seen a ghost! His forehead was not too broad, but the receding hairline gave a false impression. Deep-set eyes and a long nose were two features which had passed on from one generation to the next, like some family heirloom. He paced agitatedly across the room as he called out to his wife, Sunidhi—a petite woman with an ever-smiling congenial face. She came and asked Raunak why he was feeling so restless.

"What happened? What is the bad news that you are dying to tell me?" She asked with a bemused look. Her husband had the ability to turn a slightly bad weather into the worst of storms. She was used to his panic attacks.

"Karan had called. He is in love with a Pakistani girl and intends to marry her. He is coming to India next week to seek our blessings," Raunak told her as if just by telling her, half the problem would be resolved.

"What? A Pakistani? Has he gone mad?" Now, even Sunidhi was worried. It could not have been worse. For years, they all had been pressurizing Karan to get married and settle down, but he would not listen. They had more or less reconciled to the fact that he might not marry. Many youngsters were not marrying these days. That was still acceptable. But marrying a Pakistani? Impossible in this household!

Raunak and Sunidhi had no children of their own, and they had raised Karan since he was two years old. Karan's father, Kaushal, was Raunak's elder brother, but it was Raunak who had shouldered all the family responsibilities. Kaushal had joined the army, fresh out of college, and after that, there were only the occasional visits. After three years of marriage, when Karan was just two years old, his wife had died when a missile hit the jeep in which she was travelling to join her husband. Kaushal had been posted at the border then. He was supposed to go to the station to pick her up but due to some emergency, he could not go and instead, had sent the vehicle. Both the occupants, the driver and his wife, had died on the spot.

Young Karan, who was with his uncle Raunak and aunt Sunidhi, did not even understand what had happened. His father did not remarry but devoted his entire life to his country instead. The enemy country had devoured his wife, and when war broke out in 2028, he wanted to teach them a lesson. He was captured and was made to go through living hell.

He somehow managed to escape from the captivity and was awarded the Param Veer Chakra for his gallantry and for saving many lives.

He was a changed man. The war had destroyed whatever was left of him. He was now a bitter man, living only with the hope of seeing Pakistan destroyed.

Even to think that his son wanted to marry a Pakistani girl was an unpardonable offence. It was impossible! Raunak always felt that being a single child of three parents, Karan was actually pampered too much for his own good.

Even as a child, Karan was very determined. Raunak remembered how when Karan was around nine years old, he had asked for a laser gun. Sunidhi had put her foot down and refused to buy it for him. She was against any sort of violence and arms. She always gave the example of the U.S., which faced a civil war-like situation only because they had a very liberal gun policy that glorified keeping personal weapons.

Karan would have none of it. He wanted the gun and that was it. Even though he was too young to understand the implications, he knew it was a war of strength between him and his aunt. He gave up food and did not eat for two days. Finally, they had to give in to his demands.

The only person he was in awe of was his father. He hero-worshipped him and would always look for ways and means to gain his approval. Whenever his father was home on leave, Karan would be on his best behavior.

So, it was strange that in spite of knowing how dead against Pakistan his father was, he wanted to marry a Pakistani girl!

Sunidhi tried to reassure her husband saying, "Don't worry, we will talk sense into him when he comes." But in her heart, she had a foreboding for she knew that as difficult as it was to force Karan to take any decision, it was almost impossible to make him change his mind once he had decided.

She could see the storm brewing not too far away.

Karan felt a warmth wash over him as he landed at the Delhi airport. Every time he touched his home soil, the feeling would overwhelm him. There was something about homecoming that pulled at your heartstrings and would get even the toughest of men misty-eyed.

After bidding an emotional farewell to Fiza, he had taken a flight to Delhi. Fiza had wanted to get married right away without bothering about the people back home. Karan managed to convince her that it would not be right. There could not be any future for them if they did not connect with their past. Both their families would have to be convinced to agree to this marriage.

Karan wanted a big fat Indian wedding, whereas Fiza wanted a simple court marriage. They decided to settle these issues later. Firstly, it was important to get their families to agree to this union. Even though he knew in his heart that his father would be a tough nut to crack, he did not share this with Fiza. He did not want to scare her by telling her how vehemently his father hated Pakistan and all Pakistanis.

His father used to stay with his brother and his wife in the same parental house they had lived in all their lives. In the course of time, a lot of development had taken place and the house had also been renovated and given a modern look.

Chandni Chowk still retained its age-old charm though. All the development work had been planned in such a way so as not to affect the timeless beauty of the place. The place had a soul, and it remained intact even with the passage of time.

Uncle had sent his car to pick him up. Karan hugged the driver, Ramlal uncle, as he called him. He had been with them for many years now. He had been a *jawan* working under his father, whose life his father had saved. He refused to part with him and coaxed him into giving him a job as his driver after he took voluntary retirement from the army.

Ramlal's eyes were misty as he patted Karan on his shoulders and said, "The house becomes home when you are here. We all miss you so much and your father misses you the most."

Karan knew it was not true. His father was too busy in his own world to miss anyone. He perhaps never missed having a wife either.

They wanted to avoid the traffic so they took the longer route. The car was on the Moti Bagh road when suddenly it came to a halt with a screech.

Karan had been busy on his phone, and so, he did not see exactly what had happened, but their car had hit a biker who had taken a sudden right turn. The rider fell on the road and was trying to get up on her feet. She was a young woman, perhaps in her twenties. She was injured, but thankfully not seriously. She seemed to be in pain, and her ankle was caught under the bike. Karan got out of his car.

Onlookers started to gather, looking for a roadside drama, but she promptly told everyone that she was fine and they need not stand there. Karan helped get her foot out from beneath the bike and also helped her stand. Ramlal arranged for the bike to be taken away. They both seated the girl in their car to take her to the hospital. Since it was all her own mistake, the girl was not complaining, but it was their moral duty to help her.

In the hospital, the doctors said that she was lucky that she had escaped only with minor injuries. The ankle was sprained and it needed to be bandaged.

After the bandaging was done, the girl thanked Karan for his help. Karan offered to drop her at her place. She accepted politely and got into the car.

"I am Anu. I live in Saket," she introduced herself.

"Glad to meet you Anu, but I would have preferred if it had not been like this where you had to throw yourself in front of my car to meet me!" Karan said with his usual sense of humor. "By the way, I am Karan and I live in London, which to me is the second-best place in the world. When I am not in London, I am in Chandni Chowk in Delhi which happens to be the best place there can be."

Anu broke out into laughter. "Next time, I promise it will not be like this."

She took out her visiting card from her *jhola* and offered it to Karan.

"Oh, you are an activist, it seems," he said.

"Well, is there anything wrong in being an activist? I prefer to call myself a social worker though," she said.

"Not at all. Only, people like you have always fascinated me. I always wondered how a person could be so devoted to an idea or a thought and devote their whole life to it," he said honestly.

"These things cannot be taught or learnt. It just happens. Like love. Perhaps one day you will also be so enamored by a person or an idea that you would do anything. Who can say?" Anu smiled at him.

"Yes, indeed. Who can say what will happen in the next moment? When I landed, I had no clue that such an attractive lady would choose my car to throw herself at" Karan said. "You owe me a coffee. Call me when you are in a position to give me a ride on your black beauty which you just crashed," he teased her with a smile playing at the corner of his mouth.

"You bet! Both of us will be as good as new by tomorrow. So expect a call from me, and I will treat you to not only coffee, but also *paranthas*," she smiled back.

The air was thick with tension in the Thakur residence. Karan had just announced his intention of marrying a Pakistani girl.

His father's face had gone red with anger. He was sitting on the sofa with his uncle beside him. Sunidhi aunty was in the kitchen which was just adjacent to the living room.

"How could you even think of such a thing? You know what that country has done to us. You know what its people have done to us. How can you even think of any kind of association with a Pakistani, let alone marry a Pakistani?" Kaushal shook his head as if in amazement.

"Papa, Fiza is a wonderful girl, warm and genuine. I love her and want to marry her. Our marriage has nothing to do with our nationalities. She happens to be a Pakistani, but so what?" Karan sounded defiant.

"She is a Pakistani. That is the only thing wrong about her." His father shook his head. He was trying his best not to lose his cool.

"Yes, India and Pakistan have always been hostile to each other. It is high time we stop this animosity." Karan tried to talk to him in the softest voice possible. He did not want to sound obstinate or rude to his father.

He continued, "She is the girl whose life I had saved during the riots in 2030. I had no idea that our meeting was predestined. Now I know, and am very sure in my mind that I will marry her. I need your blessings," Karan spoke in a gentle yet firm voice.

"And I am very sure that I will not allow a Pakistani girl in my family. You are free to marry anyone in this world, even a man, if you want, but not a Pakistani," his father said with equal determination.

"Papa, you know me. When I want something, I get it. I want to marry Fiza with your blessings, and that is how it will be," Karan said, looking straight into his father's eyes.

"How could you even think of this? Have you forgotten that Pakistan was responsible for your mother's death? Have you forgotten what that country did to your father?"

"I know that both India and Pakistan has been responsible for many deaths across the border. It's not the country or the countrymen, but the politicians and the bureaucrats who are responsible for all the hatred and war. This way, our generation had no choice. We were handed this hatred for Pakistan as our inheritance; similarly, their youth have also gotten this as a gift from their previous generations," Karan was now emotionally charged. He had never thought about all this earlier, and he had never thought he would be speaking to his father like this.

"Oh, your generation got this "hatred" as inheritance, is it? Who is forcing you to carry on the legacy? You can disown the inheritance and write your own story. You need not be forced to carry on this legacy of hatred. Make peace with Pakistan; see if there would be foolish people like you on their side who would want peace. There would be none! I tell you, none! It's only in our country that we harbor idealists and liberals who talk the language of peace and have intentions to shower love upon a country that understands only war.

"Many leaders had tried to bring peace and harmony between the two countries. Some had their own axe to grind while some had genuine concern. None succeeded, for the intentions of Pakistanis were never good. In the garb of peace talks, they are only looking for more means to put India down or attack us whenever they get a chance." His father was clenching the armrests of the sofa as he spoke.

Karan did not remember when he had last had such a long and heated conversation with his father; perhaps never. Most of his communication got done through his uncle. But this was a matter of ideology. The more he was speaking, the clearer he was becoming in his mind. His uncle was looking very uncomfortable at the way the conversation was proceeding, but he knew better than to open his mouth when both the father and the son were so agitated.

"Papa, all those peace initiatives that you are talking about, we have also read in our history books. Prime Minister Bajpai had tried it in 2001 and Modi in 2016, amongst many others. You are right, none succeeded. The reason was that the initiative was from the political leaders, not from common public. The common man does not want war. Not in India, not in Pakistan, not in any corner of the world," Karan tried to put forth his argument.

"So why do you not try as a common man? How do you think people will reciprocate to you handing them an olive branch? They will reciprocate with more hatred than you can ever imagine," his father continued in his agitated state. "Yes, it's a good idea. You never believed in anything without trying it out for yourself. Yes, you can try for a peace initiative. Who knows, you might even succeed," he mocked him.

"Papa, what has this to do with my marriage?" Karan tried to bring the discussion back on track. He was still trying to reason with him using logic. His father would have none of it. He was beyond logic. He was impressed with this challenge he had thrown to his son.

"Ok. So you want my blessings for this marriage? You shall have it, provided there is peace between the two countries. But no, merely that will not be proof enough. They are good at masquerades. They will pretend to be friendly and will stab you in the back. The only way to be sure is to unite!

Yes, why not? India and Pakistan were one country less than a hundred years ago. If the common people in both countries want peace and harmony, why not get united? If what you say is true, then there should not be much resistance to unity.

It is October 2046 now. In ten months' time, both the countries would be celebrating 100 years of their respective independence. What better way than to be one again? It's my promise to you. If India and Pakistan become one again by August 2047, you will have my blessings for the marriage.

"It's my challenge to you. If you love this girl so much, and if you think that your generation wants peace, then prove me wrong and unite India and Pakistan."

His father was almost shivering, whether with anger or with excitement it was difficult to make out.

Karan was stunned. The discussion had taken an entirely new direction; India and Pakistan united? Was he joking? Why did his father not refuse straightaway instead of putting forth this impossible condition!

Karan was too overwhelmed by all this, and he quietly left the room, leaving behind an agitated old man and a man who was as perplexed as him.

He went to his room and lay down on his bed. He closed his eyes and tried to calm his mind, but his father's words kept ringing in his ears.

'Unite India and Pakistan? The old man has gone senile! He posed an impossible condition that could never be achieved,' he thought.

He opened his eyes and looked at the showcase on the front wall. It was full of trophies. He had won most of them in debates in schools and colleges. The biggest trophy in the showcase was the one he had won in a speech contest in his college. The title of his speech was, "Impossible is a word in a coward's dictionary." He won the contests because of two reasons. Firstly, he was a very good orator and had a tremendous stage presence, and secondly, he spoke only on topics which he truly believed in. He always felt that when one speaks from the heart, it is received well.

Since when did he start thinking of something as 'impossible'? When did he turn into a coward?

He lay there on the bed, his mind in turmoil, and then he called up London.

Next morning, Karan went to Lodhi Garden for a walk. This was one of his favorite places. For years, Lodhi Garden was a place where many people, from different walks of life—some sporty, some lazy, some young and some not so young—came for morning walks.

In spite of having access to modern running tracks, many still favored the age-old tradition of morning walks. Many health freaks came for the walk wearing oxygen masks. Of course, the air quality had become poor and this was a safe option.

Karan visited this park once in a while, even though it was at quite a distance from his house, and there were many parks in proximity to his place. This park had a charm of its own, and it had class. It also had a beautiful restaurant called The Garden, which was his favorite.

Karan had come here today to ponder over the sudden twist of events that had taken place. After a run in the park, he sat down on a bench thinking about the discussions of the previous evening.

Though he had expected that his father would disapprove, he did not think that he would be so dead against the idea. He had hoped to convince him and get him to agree to this marriage.

His father's words were ringing in his ears. "It's my challenge to you. If you love this girl so much and if you think that your generation wants peace, then prove me wrong and unite India and Pakistan."

It was true that the common masses on either side of the border wanted peace. There had been a lot of bloodshed and lives had been lost on both sides of the border. People were sick of the everyday bombings and the act of putting the blame on the other side. God only knew what was true and what was fabricated.

Karan had met many Pakistanis in London, and his flat-mate was a Pakistani too. They were also of the opinion that this feud between the two countries was being nurtured by the political parties for their own gains.

But uniting the two countries, which had separated a hundred years ago? That was so ridiculous that he would have been laughing at the idea had his father not been so serious; ridiculous, but not impossible.

Ever since he was a child, Karan had to be goaded into doing something. He did not have a firm opinion about anything. But if he set his mind on anything, and especially, if he was challenged, there was nothing that could stop him.

He was in a fix as to how to react to this challenge. The point was not if he could marry Fiza. He could always marry her even without his father's blessings. It was now a matter of being right. He knew he was right and that his father was being a bit too prejudiced. But how should he tackle this situation, which had become quite tricky now?

Last night, he had spoken to Fiza and told her about his conversation with his father. She had laughed at the idea of the two countries uniting. "Your father is very smart," she said. "He knows that this is impossible, and that is why he has put forth this condition."

"But Fiza, is it really impossible?" he asked.

"Karan, are you serious? Of course! It is not only impossible, but it is also absurd." She had laughed at his proposal cake question. He had joined in her laughter, but there was something nagging at the back of his mind —a feeling that he could not quite comprehend, a thought that was not very clear.

Sitting on a bench in the park, he tried to gather his thoughts.

Nelson Mandela, who was a South African anti-apartheid revolutionary, political leader, philanthropist and President of South Africa, had said, "It always feels impossible, until it is done."

Things which felt impossible a few decades ago were a reality today. Who would have thought that humans would be landing on the moon? Who would have thought that it was possible to be with a person living hundreds of miles away? Through virtual reality, you could talk to the person as if you were sitting across a table. Impossible becomes possible only when you try.

Impossible is a word in a coward's dictionary, was what Karan had believed in. Last night, he had asked himself if he had really become a coward.

No, he was not a coward. The belief and efforts determine the outcome. If no one had thought out of the box, discoveries and inventions would not have happened. What people considered as impossible till a few years back was a reality today.

He was wrong in thinking that it was an impossible idea. Nothing is ever impossible. The more he thought about it, the more confident he felt.

He might not succeed, but someone might – maybe not next month, not next year, but sometime in the future. More importantly, if through his efforts he managed to even bring peace between the two countries, he would have achieved a major victory. Who knows, his father might then relent and give his blessings to the marriage.

An idea, when backed by belief, can change the world.

Karan looked at his watch. He had been sitting here for more than two hours. In these two hours, he had made up his mind. He would take up the challenge. He started his car and drove like a man with a mission, reaching home in barely twenty minutes.

With a determined look on his face, he went to his father's room. His father was sitting on the terrace adjoining his room, sipping his tea.

"I have decided to take up your challenge, papa. From tomorrow, I will start working towards it," he said. He turned around and walked out of the room, not glancing at the old man who was left stunned and speechless.

As he was stepping out of the room after accepting what was perhaps the biggest challenge of his life, his phone rang. It was the girl on the bike who had almost come under his car, Anu.

He took the call. She was calling from her office perhaps. She had a cup of coffee in front of her and seemed so bright and active, so early in the day.

"What's up, mate?" He asked.

"I have a peace rally in a college today, and so I started early. How about having a late lunch today? Say around 2 p.m.?" She asked.

"Why not? I could do with some company," he replied. "Planning to come to this part of Delhi?" He asked.

"No, somewhere in the south would be better," she replied.

"In that case, why not meet at The Garden in Lodhi Garden? The weather is just perfect, and I love that place."

"Suits me; it is not far from where I am. See you there at two in the afternoon then. Bye," she said and hung up.

Karan found Anu waiting for him as he entered the restaurant. It was a pleasant surprise to see that she had chosen his favorite cabana. It was in the far corner of the restaurant. This place had an open garden where tables were laid, as well as a covered seating area. People preferred sitting outside when the weather was good. In the evening too, this place looked beautiful with bright, colored lanterns lighting up the trees. He always got a good feeling when he came to this place. He went forward and embraced her, kissing her on her cheeks.

She laughed. "It's good to see you. I have been thanking my stars that I came under your car the other day," she said.

"Me too. Someone else would have dragged me to the police station!" He smiled back.

"No, certainly not! It was my mistake, but we can save the niceties for later. I am famished. When I said 'a late lunch', I meant lunch and not tea." She pointed at the watch with a reproaching look.

'Yeah, sorry I got late," he said as he sat down beside her on the white mattress of the cabana. The lovely yellow cushions were well-paired with the light-blue color of the tent.

The waiter came to take their order, and Karan ordered his favorite martini with grilled tofu and brown rice. Anu ordered a red sauce whole wheat pasta and went through the bar menu for ordering the drink.

 "I will have First Love," she said, pointing at the menu — a cocktail of sparkling wine with gin and cherry liqueur.

 "Oh, you are a romantic!" He remarked.

 "Which girl isn't?" She retorted with a smile.

As they waited for the food and drinks to arrive, she started to talk about the different projects she was working on for world peace, especially about peace between the two enemy countries.

Karan was reminded of the events that had unfolded the day before, a conversation that had shaken up the world around him. He suddenly sat up straight and interrupted her as she was speaking.

"I have read that everything happens for a reason, and everyone you meet has a role to play in your life. I am starting to believe this," he said.

"Why? What happened?" She asked.

"I know now why you fell in front of only my car. I know now why you called up this morning. I know now why we met," he said. "Girl, you and I together are going to make history!" He caught hold of her hands and kissed her palms.

"Explain yourself, young man, before you kiss another part of my body!" She tried to make light of the situation.

"Don't laugh. I will explain. Promise not to laugh after I finish either," he said, and went about explaining everything — from the day he had met young Fiza in Chandni Chowk to the conversation with his father about uniting India and Pakistan.

Meanwhile, the food had arrived but neither of them was paying any attention to the lunch spread. Anu was listening to him with rapt attention.

 "What do you think?" He asked her after he had finished.

She was very quiet, thoughtful and pensive.

"I will be honest. The idea is absurd and highly unlikely" She paused. "But all great ideas sound stupid at first" She completed.

"Yes, that's what I think. It is so strange and fantastic. Who knows? Perhaps, it might turn into reality." As Karan spoke, he started to gain clarity about his thoughts.

The more they discussed, the clearer his vision became. As dusk started to fall and the restaurant geared up to prepare for the dinner ahead, Anu glanced at her watch and remarked that they should be leaving. They decided to meet the next day in her office and discuss the plan further.

"I am so happy that I met you," he said as he kissed her again on her cheeks to bid goodbye.

"It was destined," she said, and waved at him as she kick-started her black panther.

As they both went their own way, they had no idea that this evening would change the path of their destiny. They had just started talking about a wind of change, not knowing that soon this wind would take the shape of a storm and change forever not only their lives, but also the future of two nations.

The next day, Karan went to Vivek's house, which was just a ten-minute walk from his own place. Vivek's father was sitting outside on the terrace, smoking a cigarette, while his mother was in the living room, entertaining some of her friends.

They both hugged Karan as he touched their feet. They loved him like their own son, and the fact that he had had a childhood sans his biological parents also added to their affection towards him.

"Your friend is still in bed. Go and wake him up. He will be thrilled to see you," aunty said.

Karan climbed up the stairs to Vivek's room which was on the first floor.

Vivek's room was done up in a crème color theme. There was a large bed in the middle of the room and a large white wall on one side that doubled up as a screen. The other side had a glass door, and one could see the hustle and bustle of the city from there. A beautiful wooden chest, which was an antique piece, was to the left of the bed. This contained many toys with which Karan and Vivek had played as kids. There were many photographs on top of it.

This was the room where Karan had spent so many nights as a teenager. Vivek and he had played hide and seek and all kinds of boyish games. They had played virtual games when they were slightly older. They had talked about girls and experimented with a lot of stuff here. They had laughed and cried together. Yes, this room was full of memories for him; it had a soul of its own.

Indeed, Vivek was still asleep when he entered. Karan jumped on the bed and pulled off the soft quilt under which he was snuggled. Vivek woke up with a start.

"Karan! You never told me you were coming!" he screamed and tried to playfully hit him on his face. Karan knew this was coming and ducked just at the right time to avoid the blow.

"I wanted to surprise you," Karan grinned.

"Well, that you never fail to do." Vivek made a face. "That is what you are good at, giving surprises. Doing the unexpected," he did not stop complaining.

Vivek had been extremely put off when Karan had decided to go to London. Vivek had studied journalism, and his father owned a publishing house. So, it suited them both well. He had joined his father's business, and consequently, started writing for many newspapers and blogs. Vivek had wanted Karan to stay in Delhi and join his business as a partner. If not that, he at least, wished Karan would stay in the city and not sever the bond they shared by going off to a foreign country. But Karan had decided to go and that was that. Despite this, their bond was as strong as ever.

"Ok. So what's happening with Fiza?" Vivek asked. "When are you getting married? I am sure uncle will not agree to this marriage, so what have you planned?" He bombarded Karan with a barrage of questions.

"Relax. I am here to tell you all that," Karan tried to cut him short. He too climbed up on the bed, sat down and pulled a pillow onto his lap as he started to share with his best friend everything that had happened in the last few days.

As Karan started talking, a strange look came on Vivek's face. The corner of his mouth was twitching in a funny way.

Karan knew that look and said, "Don't you dare laugh, Vivek. I am serious."

At this, Vivek burst out laughing, and it was as if a dam had burst. He was unstoppable. He laughed and rolled to and fro on the bed. He actually held on to his stomach as if it was hurting with so much laughter.

Karan was furious. He punched his friend on his face, and this time, Vivek wasn't quick enough to duck.

"Ouch! That hurt," he exclaimed.

"Good. Now listen. I am serious. Let's discuss. What makes you think it is a funny idea? Even if it is, mostly all great ideas sound funny at first. The Wright brothers were considered crazy because they had thought of something no one had ever thought of before — flying. People must have laughed at Columbus the way you are laughing at me now, when he first proposed that the earth was round and not flat. See, any genius idea is always scoffed at," Karan tried to convince Vivek.

"Ok," Karan said, "I will be honest. I don't see the union of Pakistan and India happening practically ever in the future. But where is the harm in trying? My father has challenged me to do this. Most likely, I will not succeed, but at least, I will set the ball rolling. The new generation wants peace. We all agree to this. Perhaps, it will be a trigger point for the youth today, and they will actually start thinking about it. Today's youth are tomorrow's policy makers, aren't they?

"And even if nothing like this happens, my father will see how sincerely I tried to do what he asked me to do, and he will certainly give his blessings on this marriage. This is all I expect to gain out of this. You know how much his approval means to me."

Vivek was now listening to him seriously. There was this look on Karan's face which he recognized. The look of when he had already made up his mind about something. There was no point trying to dissuade him now.

"*Yaar*, I have come to you for your support. Are you with me on this or not?" Karan asked, stretching out his hand towards Vivek, palm upwards.

Vivek looked at him, in all seriousness this time. "*Saale*, if you ask me to give my life for you, I will do that with a smile. You know that. What is Pakistan? I will get you Pakistan on a platter," he put his hand in Karan's, pulled him closer and hugged him.

"No, I don't want Pakistan on a platter. 'Can India and Pakistan reunite?' is the crux of the matter." Karan played their childhood rhyming game.

"Once you set your mind, you can get the moon; Now get off my back, you goon!" Vivek shouted as he threw a pillow at Karan and ran to the washroom before Karan could retaliate.

LONDON

Fiza was having trouble sleeping properly. It was after many months that she was experiencing this bout of insomnia again. Before meeting Karan, she had frequently faced this problem, and would often pop a pill to sleep. But her relationship with Karan had been so therapeutic that she had started sleeping well. On some rare days, if she had trouble sleeping, Karan would cradle her head in his arms, running his fingers through her hair, humming some soft tune, and before long, she would slip into a deep sleep. She often wondered how he had such immense maternal instincts in him. He behaved like a mother hen sometimes. It made her feel that perhaps Allah knew that she was a motherless child who had never been pampered by anyone in her life. So, he ensured that she got someone who would actually spoil her by heeding to all her whims and fancies and giving her all the motherly love that was denied to her in her childhood.

But today, her conversation with Karan had disturbed her. She did not like the way things were progressing. He had told her that whereas he did not expect his father to agree amicably to the match, he certainly had not expected such an extremely negative response.

The recent turn of events had caught both of them by surprise. Uniting India and Pakistan! Had the old man become senile?

It was an absurd thought.

The problem was that Karan had also started thinking about it. He was telling her about some girl he had met, who was also running an NGO, working towards peace between the two countries. Karan had started to think about seriously working towards the challenge given by his father. Of course, he also knew that nothing would come out of it, but he hoped this would make his father change his mind.

Fiza did not like this development. This meant Karan would not be coming back to London immediately. She was already missing him terribly. In a short span of around six months, he had become an integral part of her life.

He wanted her to go to Pakistan and start working on the same mission. Of course, she refused. He knew how she disliked politics and all such public groups. So he did not insist. But he did ask her to tap all her friends and contacts who wanted peace between India and Pakistan and to get him connected to them. His own flat-mate at London, Riyaz was from Lahore, and he was very excited about the idea. Karan had already started garnering support.

Fiza did try to dissuade Karan. She also said that she didn't mind not getting married, and they could continue living together forever. He would have none of it. Then she extracted a promise from him that whatever happened, her name should not get dragged into any of this. Her aunt was a public figure in Pakistan and had political ambitions too. She did not want her aunt to be affected in any adverse way.

Fiza tossed and turned on the bed for a long time, and when sleep still eluded her, she finally popped a pill and waited for the darkness to engulf her.

NEW DELHI

They had their first meeting in United Coffee house in Connaught place. A series of meetings would follow in the coming months.

Karan had chosen this place because it had a history of its own. He was fond of all places that had a character. Somehow, he had a feeling deep in his heart that he was setting into motion something which would change the future of the two nations. Well, it wasn't exactly a feeling, just a sixth sense, maybe. The same way he had always felt that he would someday meet the girl from Pakistan whom he had helped years ago in Chandni Chowk.

United Coffee House was founded in 1942, the year of the Quit India movement. It was opened with an aim to bring the diverse characteristics of Delhi under one roof and offered an environment where the clients could sit, relax, interact and have intellectual discussions. Throughout its long history, this café has been crowded with artists, lawyers, journalists, businessmen, philanthropists, politicians and intellectuals from all walks of life. It has been a mute witness to many great ideas germinating from these tables.

Anu was accompanied by two people from her team. Sudha was a young girl and was leading the fundraising team, and Sumit was the media head of her NGO.

Vivek had also roped in two people. Manpreet Singh was an editor from his publishing house, and his friend, Iqbal Khan was a freelance journalist.

Karan had asked his family driver, Ramlal uncle, to also attend the meeting. He too had lost his daughter in one of the bomb blasts and was a staunch supporter of non-violence and peace.

They were eight people in all, and hence, they chose a large, round table. They placed their orders for coffee, and then Karan spoke about the purpose of the meeting.

He started with how the idea had started and went on to speak about what he expected to gain from this.

"Friends, I will be honest with you. All this is for my personal gain. I am very well aware that the idea of uniting India and Pakistan sounds like a pipe dream, but I have a feeling that even if we are not able to bring about what we have set to achieve, we will at least be able to bring peace between the two nations. We may not achieve the union of two warring countries, but we may succeed in these two nations becoming friendly towards each other.

"The Partition did not happen in a day or in a month. It took a lot of time and extracted more than its pound of flesh. Similarly, what we are striving to achieve will take time and might not happen by the 100th year of partition, but at least we would have sown the seeds."

He looked at Anu and continued, "My chance encounter with Anu also seems to be a part of the bigger plan that the universe has for me. The turn of events all seem to be following a perfectly laid out orchestration, and I have a feeling that we are the lead actors in the drama that will unfold, a drama that will change the course of history."

At this, Anu could not help herself and started clapping. All the others followed. Karan now pointed towards Anu, "Perhaps you would like to add something?" He asked.

Anu pretended to take an imaginary mike from Karan's hands. She cleared her throat and burst into laughter.

"Well, please don't be offended by my laugh, Karan. It is not that I am laughing at your idea. I think it is a great idea. I was just imagining ourselves going down in history, and I couldn't help laughing. A step that was taken to win the hand of a lover might bring love and peace between the two countries. Who knows? Nothing is impossible. Even though I agree with Karan that the reunion of India and Pakistan seems like a pipe dream, I also feel that most world-changing inventions and discoveries were laughed at initially when they were conceived. I think we should work towards uniting the two nations and not just talk about peace and harmony. All my life, my team and I have worked towards bringing peace; now we will work towards undoing the wrong that was done almost a hundred years ago."

This time, Karan started to clap and the others followed. Anu now pretended to pass on the imaginary mike to Vivek.

Vivek played along with her and pretended to be talking on the mike. "Everyone has a reason for joining. My reason is very simple. I cannot say no to my friend. Thank God, he did not ask me to jump from the balcony. I would have done that too," he said and smiled.

"*Beta*, I think jumping off of the balcony would be easier," Ramlal quipped, and everyone laughed.

Iqbal, who was a freelance journalist, then started on a serious note. The imaginary microphone was forgotten.

"Friends, I have a degree in Indian History, and the freedom struggle was my main subject. I have done a lot of research on the partition of India. Partition was a mistake that our ancestors made, and we have been paying the price for it all these years. It suited the British to divide us, otherwise India would have been a mammoth force to reckon with. I have written a lot about this in my blogs and have also published many papers on it. I have travelled widely across both India and Pakistan and have had the good fortune of meeting many like-minded people of all age groups. My findings and observations tell me that most of the youth across both sides of the border want peace and harmony. People are sick of wars, and even when there is no war, the threat of a war always looms above our heads. It's the politicians who are running their political parties by feeding it with the fuel of hatred and intolerance. Believe me, this is a fuel which is slowly burning the very warehouse in which it is stored.

I feel deeply about the subject, so pardon my long lecture, but the truth is that when my friend Vivek discussed this project with me, I just pounced upon this idea. Why worry whether we will reach the destination or not? The path would be challenging enough; let's enjoy our journey. Let's aim for the moon; who knows, we might reach the stars," Iqbal ended by quoting a *sher*,

"Udaan uchi laga parinde, to kya jo tere par chhote hain

Kya pata kisi ki dua hi tere par ban jaye"

There was pin drop silence in the room when he finished. Then the jolly sardar, Manpreet, broke the silence by breaking into an applause, "*Oye, Khush kar ditta yaar,*" he said.

Karan then told everyone about his roommate, Riyaz, who was from Pakistan. Riyaz was a staunch supporter of peace and he always said that if India had not been divided in 1947, we would have become the most powerful country by now. Karan promised to talk to him and see if something along the same lines could be started there in Pakistan. A similar movement across the border would definitely have a better impact.

Till the late hours of the evening, they sat discussing the new and untrodden path that they had chosen for themselves. They all had their own reasons for choosing to travel on this path, and they were all excited and anxious about the challenges that lay ahead. Whether their mission would be a success or failure was something that did not matter much; what mattered was that they would be doing something that they all believed in, and they could not wait to begin this new adventure.

The headquarters of Hindu Maha Morcha was in a farmhouse in Chhatarpur. A meeting of all the executive members was going on inside the big conference hall. Prof Tyagi was chairing the meeting.

There had been a recent spate of violence in a village in the Muzaffarnagar district of Uttar Pradesh. Ten members of a Hindu family had been burnt alive in that village where the Muslims were in majority.

The crime was being investigated now, and some people were also arrested, but all this was only eyewash. These interreligious feuds and riots had become a common phenomenon these days, especially in Muslim-dominated pockets.

No concrete action was ever taken to stop or prevent these riots because these villages were considered to be a major vote-bank by all political parties. Most of the political parties wanted to appease them. The party which had come to power promising to bring the lost glory back to the Hindus, had also not been able to do anything substantial for the Hindus so far. Such was the compulsion of power that the parties forgot all that was promised in their manifestos after they got elected to power. The only thing that mattered after coming to power was how to retain this power. Prof Tyagi was disillusioned with the party, even though there had been a time when he was a strong supporter of the party.

It was after one such major Hindu-Muslim riot in 2037, which had spread to many places throughout the country, that the Hindu Maha Morcha was formed. It was founded by a group of Professors from Benares Hindu University. Prof Tarun Tyagi was one of the founder members. The objective of the Maha Morcha was to protect the rights of the Hindu community and to ensure that they did not end up becoming a minority in a country in which they were once a majority.

The Muslim community, which was considered a minority, was actually in majority in many places. In the census of 1951, the Hindus had a population of 84% and Muslims 9.8%. Between then and now, the Muslim population had more than doubled and was at 22%, whereas Hindus formed 75% of the total population. The way this demographic ratio was changing so rapidly was alarming, but no one in the political circles seemed to be bothered about it. That was why intellectuals from the Hindu community had to unite and work for protecting their own interest. HMM was looked down upon by many for being a sort of militant Hindu Organization. Prof Tyagi never shied away from answering such accusations. "If Muslims can have militant organizations, why not Hindus?" He would ask. Hundreds of years ago, Charles Darwin had proposed the theory of survival of the fittest. This held true even today, he would say.

After the incident of mass massacre in the Chhabua village of Muzaffarnagar district, he had immediately called for the emergency meeting. An action plan was drawn to propagate the news of the incident across the length and breadth of the country. It was already late, but it was better late than never for the Hindus to unite against the atrocities committed by the other community wherever they were in the majority.

Prof Tyagi had made an emotional and inspiring speech, which gave everyone present there an adrenaline rush. Sooraj was no exception. In fact, it was after seeing such videos that Sooraj had joined this Morcha. It was through his commitment and dedication to the cause that he speedily rose up the party ranks, and he was now a member of the executive committee.

Sooraj was the spokesperson of the party, and even though most of the communication was done by Prof Tyagi himself, Sooraj participated in many talk shows to put across the viewpoint of his party. The communication with the media and also the general public was done by him and his team. Of course, other than his official duties, he also was considered to be the right hand man of Prof Tyagi even though he was much junior to many other members, both in rank as well as in age.

Even while listening to Prof Tyagi's speech, his mind was already making points as to what he had to say to the media, and he was drafting the press release in his mind.

It was a sunny morning, but there was a slight nip in the air. Sunlight was streaming in through the glass windows. A sunny day never failed to lift Karan's spirits. He felt like basking under the sun. So, he went to his room, took out a book that he was reading, and also grabbed his sun cap. He then went out on the terrace and sat down on the green garden chair.

He propped his legs up on the small cane *modha,* lowered his head back on the headrest and closed his eyes. The soft rays of the sun kissed his face, and for a few minutes, he just lay there soaking in the sun. His phone rang. It was Fiza. He immediately took the call.

They spoke for some time. She told him about her work and how they were planning a new campaign for launching a new chain of hotels for a client. She had been given the responsibility of this campaign, and she was very excited about it. She would have to travel a lot. She loved to travel anyway.

Karan told her about the developments happening on his front. Fiza was very surprised to know that they had already had their first meeting. Karan told her about all the people present in the meeting, their backgrounds and their reasons for joining him.

Fiza was listening with great interest. Then suddenly, she asked, "How does Anu look like? Is she pretty?"

Karan burst out into laughter. "All the girls are the same. When I told Anu about you, she asked me the same question. I showed her your pic."

"Ok, but you still haven't answered my question," she persisted.

"Well, you can't say that Anu is beautiful, but she is attractive. I have never seen any makeup on her face. Perhaps there is a beauty in her simplicity." Karan tried to be as objective as he could.

"She sounds interesting," Fiza said. "I am going to sleep now," she said and blew him a kiss, before hanging up abruptly.

"Girls!" Karan sighed.

He opened the book to read, but his thoughts were in turmoil. So much was happening these days. He marveled at the speed with which the events had unfolded so far.

He had asked Vivek to find out the formalities of forming a society or a group. He wanted to do things properly, legally. He had no intention of landing in any legal hassle.

He told Anu to think of a name for their movement or their organization. They decided to convene the next meeting in the coming weekend. Meanwhile, all were asked to brainstorm and think of ways and means to achieve their goal. In the next meeting, the action plan had to be chalked out along with the assignment of roles and responsibilities.

Karan was lost in his thoughts when suddenly, his father entered through the terrace door and sat down on the other vacant chair beside him.

"I knocked, but you were too lost in your thoughts to hear," he explained.

"It's ok, Dad. You need not knock." Karan removed his feet from the *modha* and sat upright.

"Army ingrains in you certain conduct that become a part of you," Kaushal said. "Try as I might, I still find myself out of place in this civil society," he smiled. "So what's happening?" He asked, trying to make amends for the heated argument they had had only a few days ago.

"Nothing, Dad," he answered. He did not want to tell him about his plans when he himself was not clear about the action plan.

"Karan, do something with your life. When I was your age, I was a major in the army and was a leader of more than a hundred men. I had already fought a battle. You seem to be going nowhere in your life. I thought after doing your MBA, you would stick to a job, but you have changed three jobs in less than a year. Please become serious about something in life. It's high time." His father tried to keep the tone conversational, but Karan was aware that it was anything but that! His father was really disappointed in him. He did not stick to anything for long; no job, no interests and no ideology.

Well, perhaps if he could do something with this new mission that he was undertaking, he would be able to prove to his Dad that he was not a 'good-for-nothing' after all.

As the sun slid behind the trees in the Qutub complex, there appeared a crimson-golden hue in the sky which made the

Qutub Minar look like a blushing bride. Anu smiled at her own thoughts and continued with her sketch.

She was sitting on the green grass in a park in the Qutub Complex. She liked to go to historical places and practice her sketching. It was not only a hobby, but also a stress-buster for her.

Indian history had been her favorite subject at school. It was like reading a new story every time; so many dynasties, so many rulers, and so many stories. Stories that were woven together to create history. People lived their lives, and they might not have been aware that they were leaving behind a legacy and that their names would go down in history. The present never knows what place it is creating for itself in the future.

Anu wanted to do something which would make history, something for which people would remember her for generations to come; something that would change peoples' lives for the better.

Her NGO, Messengers of Peace, was her small step towards bringing peace in the world. She wanted this to be the stepping stone for bigger things in the future.

It was by a sheer stroke of luck, or perhaps the intervention of the universe, that she had met Karan. His idea of uniting India and Pakistan was very radical, and she could see something good coming out of it. As it was, she had needed to do some campaigning to make people notice her and create an impact. This was her opportunity.

If handled smartly, this idea had the power to create a revolution.

This was her key to the door leading to fame. Her mind was racing as she was thinking of all that she could do, all that they could do as a team. Her hand moved ferociously over the paper as she drew strong and determined strokes with her special charcoal pencil that she used for her sketches.

The sun was almost gone now, and the shadows were melting. She had planned to complete the sketch of the beautiful Qutub Minar before dark, but now it looked as if she would have to make another visit. She took the charcoal pencil and pressed it inside the bun she had shaped her hair into. Many people found it strange that she always had her pencil tucked inside her hair bun, but this gave her the freedom to sketch anywhere and anytime when something caught her fancy. Her *jhola* obviously carried many such pencils and a sketching pad.

Slinging her *jhola* across her shoulders, Anu got up and walked towards the parking. Just then, she got a call from Sumit, her media manager. He told her that the HMM had started a very aggressive hate campaign against the violence that had happened in Chhabua village. He said that there were strong chances of witnessing spurts of riots across the country.

Anu listened to him with a concerned look on her face. These various religious organizations were only making matters worse. If it was within her power, she would have banned the formation of any religious groups. They only instigated people, and what could have been merely a case of inter-family vendetta, was being given the hues of an inter-religion clash.

'I will have to meet with their spokesperson one of these days,' she thought to herself, grimacing at the thought. They would have to increase their activities in Uttar Pradesh. She suddenly got an idea, a brainwave. "Sumit, make arrangements for my travel to Chhabua Village," she said with a smile on her face as she jumped on her black panther and kick-started it. She had gotten a brilliant idea to kick-start their own campaign. She adjusted her earphones and asked her Google Assistant to put a call through to Karan immediately.

CHHABUA
MUZAFFARNAGAR DISTRICT, UP

The house had a deserted look, and the big terrace in the front was cluttered with leaves and dust, which clearly indicated that no one had swept it for days.

A jute charpoy lay there in the middle, abandoned and full of dirt. The yellow jute had dark maroon patches on it. At three places on the terrace floor, there were circles drawn with white paint. There were faint traces of some strange color inside these circles. On closer inspection, one could make out that they were blood stains.

There were four rooms which were facing the open terrace, but all of them were locked. There was no one inside the rooms, which was evident from the fact that there was no light coming through the cracks of the window or the door. The only sign of some life inside the house came from a light which was switched on in one of the rooms in the farthest corner.

Inside the room, Ajay Pratap Singh lay on the bed staring at the ceiling with lifeless eyes. On the other side of the bed was his wife, Sunita, who was pretending to be asleep.

The soundless sobs that shook her body now and then, gave away the fact that she had not slept. Could a mother, whose children had been massacred in cold blood, sleep?

It was not even a month since that brutal act had been committed. Ajay lived with his two brothers and their families and his aged mother. They were a joint family of thirteen people. They had a large piece of ancestral land where they practiced farming. They were doing well. The younger brother, along with his family, had shifted to Lucknow a few years back but had returned to the village barely after six months. Life in the big city did not suit them.

All the children of the family were studying in the village school. Ajay's son was the eldest and he was in the twelfth standard. His daughter was a year younger and was studying in the eleventh class.

Sunita had not been keeping well for a few weeks. Even after undergoing treatment in the village hospital for more than two weeks, there was no improvement in her condition. So, they had decided to go to Lucknow to meet a specialist.

Ajay would never forget that fateful day when he returned from the city at about five in the evening. The door was open, and there were fresh, blood-stained footprints leading out of the house.

He felt his heart sink. He and Sunita rushed inside, and the sight that greeted them would haunt them for the rest of their lives. Corpses of all shapes and sizes were lying on the terrace, eleven of them. Their own son's head was severed, and it lay far away from the body. Their daughter lay next to her brother's headless body, clutching his hand. When alive, they always fought like cats and dogs, but they could not live without each other. Even in death, they were clinging on to each other. Ajay's mother must have been the first to be killed because she must have been resting on the charpoy in the terrace. Her body lay there with a big wound on the stomach.

Both the brothers must have put up a fight, for their bodies were badly dismembered. It was the youngest brother whose body was cut into at least twenty pieces. It was only because of his neon-dyed hair that he could be recognized.

Sunita lost consciousness while Ajay threw up. His legs gave way and he sank to the floor. He could barely manage to call the police, pressing the emergency number on the phone.

What happened afterwards was a blur. The police asked if they had any enemies, because a robbery was certainly not the motive behind this mass massacre.

Ajay had no enemies as such but his younger brother had one. His brother had been duped of a large amount when he had bought a house from a local person in the village, Abdul Arsad. After he had paid the token money, it was found that the house was a joint property and could not be sold by one person. His brother had wanted his money back, whereas the seller wanted to go ahead with the transaction. After trying to reason with him and even after taking the village *sarpanch's* help, when he did not return his money, his brother had no option but to lodge a complaint with the local police.

There were many threats made to him to withdraw the case. One day, Abdul had come with local goons and asked him bluntly to withdraw the FIR or else face 'dire consequences.' "You are all rats, so live like rats. Don't try to become lions, or else you will die a dog's death," he had said.

It was true that the village was actually Muslim-dominated, and there were only a few Hindu households. Even then, never in their wildest dreams had anyone thought that they would all be butchered like this.

If Ajay and his wife had arrived a few hours earlier, they would also had been dead that day.

Ajay was the only one to light the fire to eleven pyres while his wife lay admitted in the hospital.

The police had arrested Abdul and a case was registered. Ajay did not have the strength to go to the court or the police station. Some neighbors had arranged for help and some relatives from other cities had come.

After the *kriya,* they all left one by one. His wife was also discharged from the hospital. Now, two lifeless bodies were living alone in the big house.

Then, one evening, a man came from a television channel. He asked them questions and took their photos. He enquired about the nature of the murderer, especially if there was a different religious community involved or not. He asked if ever they had felt prosecuted by the majority community.

From the next day onwards, they were in the news. Many journalists and media people came day in and day out. They were the topic of debates and discussions. Many theories were going around. While most said that it was a planned crime by the Muslim community, there were some who suggested that Pakistan was behind this so that there would be riots in the country. No one ever looked at the fact that it was one criminal mind who, for his personal gains and inflated ego, had committed this mass murder. Ajay was so fed up with all the politics over his tragedy that he broke his TV set.

They were trying to somehow get their mental state back to normal, but the people would make them relive the nightmare every moment.

The car raced on the road at a speed of 110 km per hour. This was a newly constructed road, courtesy of one of the Government drives to improve the condition of the highways.

Inside the SUV, four people were sitting along with the driver. Anu and Karan were in the middle row, whereas Vivek sat in the front with Ramlal, who was driving. Sumit was in the back and was busy working on his laptop.

After receiving Sumit's call when she was at the Qutub Complex, Anu had called up Karan.

Chhabua was a must-visit place for her as it needed the healing touch of peace. It needed the balm of love on the hearts which were tormented by the feelings of revenge and hatred.

She thought this was the right time to start the campaign that Karan wanted. This place might prove to be a launch pad for his idea. When the situation is volatile and the nerves are raw, people will listen to any out-of-the-box idea, and Karan's idea was out-of-the-box, to say the least.

Karan was not very sure that the platform of communal violence would be the right one to start talking about peace, and also about an idea no one had even thought of before.

Anu, on the other hand, had full confidence in herself and thus, had managed to convince Karan to accompany her. That is how they had all ended up going to meet Ajay and his wife Sunita, who had lost eleven members of their family in a single day. Vivek knew the District Magistrate of Muzaffarnagar and had arranged a meeting with him. He also arranged for a small press conference at Chhabua because Anu had requested for the same.

They arrived at their destination at around 12:30 pm. On the way, they had stopped for breakfast at one of the roadside *dhabas*. After a heavy breakfast of *aaloo paratha* and curd, they felt full, so no one wanted to have lunch. They decided to go straight to the DM's office.

Mr Ankur Rohtagi was Vivek's father's friend, and he greeted them warmly. They sat in his cabin, and the attendant served them tea in beautiful bone china cups. Vivek introduced all of them. When he introduced Anu as the founder of the NGO, Messengers of Peace, Mr Rohtagi commented that he had heard of the NGO and that they were doing a good job.

"In a world which is getting negative with every passing day, when people are only talking of caste, creed and communal divide, when violence has become a part of our lives, it's so refreshing to see young people like yourself talking of peace," he said, shaking Anu's hand with great warmth.

Anu's face lit up on hearing such compliments. She then started sharing her thoughts on how the people of Chhabua needed the healing touch of love at this time. She spoke of her plans to have an open press conference along with a public meeting.

Mr Rohtagi was already aware of the press conference and informed them about the arrangements he had made for the same. Vivek had spoken to him about it. As for the public meeting, he had given them permission for it to be held in a nearby park. The press conference and the meeting were planned for the next morning.

So, it was decided that they would go and meet Ajay and his wife Sunita after finishing their tea.

Ajay and Sunita were already informed in advance of their arrival. Moreover, they had become used to the media attention and also to the continuous spate of visitors.

So it was not a surprise that there was a look of exasperation on Ajay's face when he opened the door of his house for them.

The DM had sent one of his officers along with them. The officer was known to the couple. He made the introductions, and they all sat down on the open terrace where some chairs had been laid out. It was obvious that the chairs did not belong to the house and had been specially arranged for this meeting.

Since Sunita had not joined the meeting, Anu enquired about her.

"Where is your wife?" She asked.

"She is not well," Ajay replied, avoiding her eyes.

"Well, if that is the case, then she can lie here," the officer said in an authoritative tone, pointing at the cot lying in the terrace.

"These people have come from Delhi and this sahib has come from London to meet both of you," he said, looking at Karan. "Please call her," he told Ajay.

Karan felt very uncomfortable and guilty. As it was, the couple was devastated after losing their family members. On top of it, every day, some people would come to ask questions which would remind them of the massacre, however hard they tried to forget it.

'Are we doing the right thing?' Karan wondered.

Ajay meanwhile called out to his wife. When Sunita entered the area, Karan felt even worse, for she indeed looked very sick. Her face was lifeless and her eyes had a vacant look. She quietly greeted everyone with folded hands and a straight face.

Karan got up from where he was sitting while Sunita sat down on the chair next to Anu. Karan sat down after she was seated.

Anu started the conversation. She put her hand on Sunita's shoulder and said, "We cannot even imagine the kind of grief you are going through, and we hate the fact that we are disturbing you in your period of mourning."

Sunita just kept staring into space.

"We want to tell you that we are with you and that we will try our best to see that the guilty are punished. But we have not come to you for this. Many people would have already promised you all this, we are sure. We have come to you because today, many political parties are using your tragedy for their political gains. They are using it to stir the religious sentiments and create political instability. Some are talking of retaliation, which means more violence. A certain section of the media is also saying that the entire massacre is a brainchild of Pakistan to start a civil war."

"Why are you here? Are you not from some political party? What is that you want to gain from our tragedy?" Sunita asked bluntly, looking Anu directly in her eyes.

Anu looked straight back. Sincerity shone from her eyes.

"No, we are not from any political party. I am from an NGO called 'Messengers of Peace,' and our aim is to bring peace and harmony in the country. The hatred, the violence and the bloodshed that is happening everywhere in the world has to stop. We are doing our little bit in making the world a better place to live in," she said.

Anu's words had a slight impact on Sunita's expressions. There was a flicker of interest on her face.

It was her husband who spoke next. "Everyone who comes here is looking for something even though they claim otherwise. What can we do for you?" He asked directly.

"I will be honest. We are here to seek your help. Even though you are in great pain, you are the people who can help save many lives. You are the people who can help bring peace," Anu said.

Sunita was now genuinely interested. "We? How?" She asked.

"Well, from what I understand about the case, it was a personal vendetta that led to this massacre, but many people are trying to give it a communal colour. Parties are instigating the Hindu community to take revenge. The situation, as you are aware, is very volatile. You can come out and say that it was actually a barbaric person and not the whole community who committed the murder. Such a person cannot follow any religion for no religion can allow such a macabre act. You have to talk about peace and not violence. You have to talk of love and not hatred. I want you to address the people tomorrow and talk of peace between the warring communities."

Everyone was listening attentively as Anu spoke, her voice, full of passion. Karan realized at that moment how deeply she was driven by the cause. Unless you sincerely believe in something, you cannot put your heart and soul into it. Anu was totally consumed by the mission she had undertaken.

The discussions moved on to what should be done and what should be spoken the next day. As the city was burning in the fire of communal violence, inside the little house, which was the epicenter of all this turmoil, a tiny group of people were talking only about peace.

It was late in the evening when they finally dispersed. The beleaguered couple was fully on board with their mission. Perhaps, they were scared of the monsters that were haunting them and so they were looking for an escape. A purpose, a mission was what they needed now to immerse themselves in.

After the meeting, the entire team went to the guest house where the DM had made arrangements for their stay. It was a modest, no-frills guest house with clean, basic rooms. They were all allotted separate rooms. The best part of the guest house was the beautifully landscaped garden at the front.

The window in Karan's room opened into the garden. After taking a bath, he sat on a chair, looking out of the window. Somehow, he felt very disturbed.

The meeting with Ajay and Sunita had been emotionally draining for him. After Anu had broken the ice, the couple had broken down and talked about their loss. They had dropped their defenses and opened their wounds for all to see. Nothing anyone could do or say would ever bring back even a fraction of what they had lost that day. Time could only give them strength to live with the pain. Contrary to the common perception, time does not really heal; it only teaches you to accept.

The sun had set. Karan wondered what the new sun would bring for him the next day. It was going to be a major event for him. He had not decided what he would say. He would jot down the points that night. He was very good at public speaking, but this was different. He was entering unknown waters, and he had no idea if he would sink or swim.

The intercom rang. It was Vivek, and he was calling Karan to the dining hall for dinner. Karan reached there to find that the entire team was already there. The dinner was laid out; a simple meal of *roti, daal, sabji* and salad. They all ate quietly. No one was in the mood for talking. They were all lost in their own thoughts.

After dinner, they all went to Vivek's room to discuss the plan for the following day. The roles were assigned. Vivek was to look after all the arrangements with the help of the DM. He was also to ensure a decent public turnout.

Iqbal, though not present, had arranged for a good number of journalists from the local, as well as the national media.

Anu was to escort Sunita and Ajay from their house to the venue.

Sumit was to manage the other administrative arrangements and also social media.

Anu, Karan and Sumit were to answer the questions from the media, whereas Sunita, Anu and Karan were to speak after the press conference was over.

It was past eleven when the discussions got over. They decided to retire for the night and went to their rooms.

Karan lay down on the bed but could not sleep. In his mind, he could hear his father saying, "It's my challenge to you. If you love this girl so much, and if you think that your generation wants peace, then prove me wrong and unite India and Pakistan!"

What had he undertaken? Forget about unifying, even peace between the two countries felt like a distant dream today! He closed his eyes and the lifeless face of Sunita flashed in his mind. He tossed and turned on the bed for some time. After another futile attempt at sleep, he got up from the bed and looked out of the window. It was a full moon night, and the park was bathed in the moonlight. The marble bench in the middle of the park was glistening. On impulse, he wore his slippers and stepped out of his room to go to the park.

As he neared the velvety green carpet, he took off his slippers and walked barefoot. He sat down on the bench and gazed at the moon. It looked so majestic. He suddenly yearned to talk to Fiza.

Back in London, sometimes, they would sit in the balcony of her flat and gaze at the moon. She would rest her head on his lap, and he would sing to her an old Hindi film song, *"Maine poochha chand se, ki dekha hai kahin, mere yaar sa haseen"* and she would listen to him with half-closed eyes, immersed in the melody of the song and the romantic ambience.

He missed Fiza. She had become an integral part of his life in a short time. He looked at the time. Fiza must be home by now. He called her. She picked up on the first ring.

"I am missing you, Karan," she said, making a sad face.

"Not as much as I am missing you," Karan replied.

Then he went on to describe the events of the day. Fiza listened with a skeptical look on her face. She was uncomfortable with the entire idea of India and Pakistan's union or even an attempted peace for that matter.

As they were talking, Karan suddenly felt a movement behind him. He turned around to see that Anu was standing there. In her pajamas, and with her hair disheveled, she was looking more like a schoolgirl rather than a girl with a mission.

"Oh, sorry. I did not realize that you were on the phone," she said, turning to go back.

"No, no, it's Fiza. Come and say hi to her," he said.

The girls met for the first time, through the phone screen, one sitting in her bedroom in London, the other in her night dress in a remote village in India.

"Good to see you, Anu," Fiza said. "Karan has spoken a lot about you."

"Oh, I hope all good," she laughed. "And I am very happy to meet the girl because of whom we are all here."

Fiza laughed a false laugh, for she was not comfortable with the reference of her involvement in the entire event which was unfolding.

"Ok! Gotta go," she said. "Meeting some friends at the bar."

She blew a kiss at Karan and waved to Anu as she disconnected the phone.

"How come you are here?" Karan asked looking at Anu.

"I saw you sitting in the park and decided to come over," she said as she sat down on the bench beside him. "She is so pretty."

"Yes, she is. She is a beauty with brains," Karan said, a hint of pride in his voice. "I am a lucky guy."

"Well, to be honest, I think she is a lucky girl," she said, looking straight into his eyes.

He did not know why, but he felt disconcerted. He looked away and said, "That's so sweet of you, Anu."

"You could not sleep?" She asked. Then, without waiting for his answer, she continued, "It's natural to be slightly nervous before any major event. This might not be a big event per se, but this might be a trigger point for bigger things to come."

She continued to speak. "Karan, I have a very strong feeling that our meeting was destined. We both are cut out for something big. My sixth sense is always very good by the way, so don't take this lightly."

Then, suddenly, she turned towards him and gave him a peck on his left cheek. "I wish you were not taken," she said with a laugh. "The two of us would have been good together."

Karan was taken aback at her frank admission, but he was quick to hide his surprise and said, "We will still be good together, Anu. Good things have already started to happen." He put his hand on top of her palm and gave it a reassuring squeeze.

"It's late. Let's try to get some sleep," he said.

"Your room or mine?" She winked at him as she laughed.

"In our separate rooms," he too laughed as he replied.

"Hey, don't be serious. I was just pulling your leg," she said.

"I know," Karan said as they started to go to their own rooms.

"Perhaps I was not. You should not be so sure," she laughed, waving at him, as she went inside her room, closing the door behind her.

Karan was left staring at the closed door, and then, he too went to his room for the much-needed sleep which had been eluding him.

It was time to start the press conference. The hall was full of people. It's amazing how much help you can garner if you know the right people. Having the District Magistrate on their side had a lot of advantages. Iqbal too had used his contacts and had lined up many people from various media houses. There were about ten or twelve people from the media, and there were more than a hundred people from different walks of life. No one knew from where Vivek had arranged the audience, but there was a decent crowd in the town hall. The stage was set. All they had to do was to start their act.

Anu had escorted Ajay and Sunita, and they were waiting in the room adjacent to the hall. Ajay was looking nervous, but Sunita was looking composed. She seemed to be unaffected by all these. She had seen so much in life that perhaps nothing affected her now.

Karan and Sumit were already on the stage. Karan was wearing a light green *kurta* and white trousers. Fiza had gifted this kurta to him on Eid. He was unexpectedly calm. Once a decision was made, he went into action mode, and all he could think about was the job in hand. He had not written any speech for the day. He had decided to say whatever came to his mind. Speaking from the heart was something he always believed in. When you say something which you have rehearsed, there are chances of making a mistake or forgetting something. When you are speaking straight from the heart, you connect better with the people. He did make an outline in his mind though, about the points he would touch upon in his speech.

Anu entered the hall along with Sunita and Ajay. Ajay sat next to Karan, and Sunita sat on his left. Anu sat on Karan's right. Sumit was standing in front of the dais. He looked at his watch and Anu gestured at him to start.

Sumit started off by welcoming the guests and the media people. Then he introduced Anu as the founder of the NGO, Messengers of Peace. He dwelled on her accomplishments and the works of the NGO. Then he invited her to the dais to speak.

"Friends," she started off, "many of you must have read the short story by O Henry. A young man was bequeathed a huge sum of money by a relative till the time he was studying. The sum was so big that it became a motivation for him to keep failing in his exams every year. He never left the college, and as a result, kept getting the money. This went on for many years till he met a girl and fell in love. He proposed marriage, but the girl refused to marry someone who was failing exams year after year so as to be eligible for his inheritance.

Now, he had to choose between a grand lifestyle with a huge sum of money and marrying the girl he loved. Of course, love won.

This is one of my favorite stories, as every time I read it, it reminds me of the power of love.

Love, they say, can conquer mountains. Love has a power that most of us cannot even fathom.

Today, we are here to witness some of its magic. When we tell you what today's meeting is all about, most of you will laugh. I have no problem with that. Laugh to your heart's content. But after that, think about what has been said. We need you to think. Only if we, today's youth, think about the current situation, we will be able to build a better future.

Before we go straight to our main story, we have before you a couple whose irreparable personal tragedy has been misused by many people and groups for their vested interests. You all must have heard of Ajay and Sunita whose entire family was butchered by a monster.

Unfortunately, some people are giving it a communal colour, trying to create mistrust and disharmony between Hindus and Muslims. People are trying to instigate Hindus into taking revenge. More violence will follow. Violence begets violence, until we put a stop to it and give back love and compassion in return, because just like violence, love begets love too.

I will not tell you this. Even if I do, you will not, or in fact, need not listen to me. But you should definitely listen to the victim who has been the target of this violence. I would like to introduce to you that woman who lost her entire family except for her husband to the most vicious of crimes. Let us listen today to what she has to say."

Without further ado, Anu passed the mike to Sunita.

Sunita did not come to the dais. She held the mike with steady hands as she looked at her husband. Ajay nodded and she looked at the audience.

 "If I could turn back the clock and change the past, I would not mind giving my life to do so," she started. "But alas, however much science has developed we still are mere puppets in the hands of God."

"I can go into the gory details of what I saw and what I felt on that fateful day we returned from Lucknow. I choose not to do that. The media has not stopped talking about it. Many people approached me to speak about it but I declined. A lot has been said already about the motive of the crime, and I know I should not remain quiet any more. Hence, I am here."

Sunita paused for a while, closing her eyes. She started again with a determined voice, "People are saying that this incident was done by a particular community to teach the other community a lesson.

No! A hundred times, no!"

This is a crime committed by a monster for his personal gains. This is a crime committed by a man who had only one motive — revenge, personal revenge! The murderer's religion has no relation with this crime. No religion teaches to kill. We have been living with Muslims in great harmony since the beginning. My best friend is a Muslim. Our close family friends are Muslims. Just because the murderer happened to be a Muslim, we should not give it a communal colour.

My loss is unbearable, but I have to live with it. I am trying to survive. But when I hear people talking about taking revenge against a particular community, I wonder why am I surviving? To be the reason for more violence, more deaths? You kill them then, they will kill you. This will continue to happen. There is no end to this revenge killing.

I am no one to tell you what to do or what not to do. You are all adults and have your own conscience. My request with folded hands is that please don't use my personal tragedy as an excuse for further killings. That ill-fated incident was due to the insanity of a mad person. A community did not kill my family, an individual did. If you want to help me, see to it that the man who did this is hanged. Don't penalize the entire community for his heinous crime." Sunita was now speaking with folded hands.

"When I think of my loss and the agony that we have gone through, I wish from the bottom of my heart that no one else should have to experience that pain. Revenge will not bring back my family, my children again. Please, I plead with you. Stop talking of revenge and hatred." Tears, which she had valiantly controlled till now, suddenly spurted from her eyes and started rolling down her cheeks.

Many eyes in the audience were moist.

Anu got up and went to Sunita to give her a comforting hug. Then she took the mike from her and spoke again.

"India had always been a country where different religions have lived in peace and harmony. If we look back in history, we will find that it was during the partition that Hindus and Muslims were taught to mistrust and hate each other. The British gave this legacy to us. When they divided the country into two, they ensured that there would always be fear and mistrust between the two communities rather than love and understanding.

But what was done was done. We can't change the past. But we can always change the future.

We can't change history, but we can definitely write our present and consequently, our future.

So now, we come to the main story. This is a story of love. This is a story about peace. This is a story about rewriting history to build a new future for two countries.

One man amongst us has a dream which most of you will laugh at when you hear. But that does not bother him. Do you know why? Because he knows that it's our duty to nurture that dream and work towards fulfilling it. If it's a dream worthy of being realized, then it will be realized. And even if it does not, it will remain an unfulfilled dream. So what? It is still our right to dream. It is those dreams that we see with open eyes that keep us awake at nights.

So, I introduce to you, a man with a unique dream, an ordinary man with an extraordinary dream for a beautiful purpose. Ladies and gentlemen, meet Karan Thakur."

Karan got up from his seat with folded hands and then slowly walked towards the dais.

"Thank you Anu, for giving me this platform, and I thank you all for coming here. As Anu has already mentioned, what I am going to say today might sound ridiculous and absurd to many; it might even sound obnoxious to some. But I will say what I have come to say anyway.

"Friends, I live in London, and there I met a beautiful and charming Pakistani girl. We fell in love; I came back to India to seek my father's blessings. My father has put forward a condition to my marrying this girl. The condition is to reunite India and Pakistan!"

The entire audience broke into laughter. Karan too laughed with them.

"As I already said, you might find it funny. Initially, even I did. Then I started thinking. It is not as outlandish as it sounds. After all, the partition of our country was something most people did not want back in 1947. But it happened due to the divide and rule politics of the British. If the enemy is united, it is formidable. The best way to defeat them is to divide them, and that's exactly what they did.

"That's what happened nearly a hundred years ago. All these years, we have been fighting wars and hating each other. But what if we had not been divided? Our country would have been a force to reckon with. Not having undergone the trauma of separation and rebuilding our respective nations from scratch after the devastation of the partition, just imagine how much we would have progressed.

"It's never too late though. The youth today wants peace. We have seen enough wars. We want love and trust between the two countries. Better still, why not see the two countries unite on our 100th anniversary of freedom and set for the world a new example of love and peace?"

This time, there was no laughter. There were many raised hands though.

"Do you have a plan, sir?" The redhead from the front row asked. Her badge said that she was from the Daily News channel.

"I do not have a detailed plan yet, but we will work something out after considering the response we get from the masses. We are going to start with a signature campaign in both the countries. My close friend, who is a Pakistani, has also joined the movement and is garnering support in Pakistan," Karan replied.

"Do you have any political support?" The youngish journalist from The Breakfast News asked.

"No, I am totally apolitical," Karan replied.

"What makes you think that the Pakistani, or for that matter even the Indian Government would even consider this proposal?" This question came from the audience.

"They might not initially, but if the public wants something, they will have to relent in the end," Karan said.

"Why would the public want this?" This came from another journalist from *The Fatafat News*.

"Because there are people like me on both sides of the border who want peace and harmony to prevail. We have no political agenda."

"Who would form the new Government?" Asked a bespectacled boy.

"I am so happy that you are even thinking to that extent. But yes, those things can be worked out," replied Karan.

A man in his mid-thirties got up from his chair. He had long hair and a beard. He shook his head to push back the strand of hair that was falling on his face, looked around the hall, and then stared straight at Karan.

"I am Rafiq Ahmed from Lahore Live channel," he said.

He again paused for impact.

"This is the stupidest idea I have ever heard in my lifetime," he continued. There was laughter again. "But sometimes, when the world is full of wisdom, one of the most unwise ideas often turns out to be the best. This sounds like a mad idea, but sometimes we all need a dose of madness in our lives. Our countries have tried everything except this. Who knows, this might turn out to be the idea of the millennium," he started to clap as he finished speaking.

There were some people from the audience who joined him.

"Thank you," Karan said. "This is just the beginning of this dream. I know we have a long way to go. I don't know if we will succeed or even come close to it. But I need your help and support. This will happen only if the public wants it. So ask yourself, do you want to give your children a better future? If yes, then please join this movement.

"The movement is called 'Let Us Be One in 2047'."

There was more applause this time.

Anu came to the stage and spoke for some more time. She thanked Ajay and Sunita for their courage and their message of love and harmony. She then thanked Karan for his out-of-the-box idea. She said that it was an idea in its nascent stage. The purpose of sharing it today was to make people think, and if they agreed with this, they could join the movement. Nothing can be achieved if it remains confined to one person, city or a country. It has to be a mass movement across both sides of the border. She thanked them for coming and requested them not only to share and spread the word but also to be a part of the movement. She shared the details for registration and also the social sites where one could register.

She smiled as she walked down from the stage after her speech and sighed in relief that their first public meeting was a success. The seed had been planted in the minds of the people. They now had to nurture it so that it could grow into a sturdy tree and bear fruits.

After thanking the DM for all his support, they went to bid goodbye to Ajay and Sunita.

Sunita hugged Anu and said, "You are doing a good job. We need more people like you."

"Thank you! I will wait for you in Delhi. Whenever you feel up to it, you can join us there. Meanwhile, you can join our movement and carry on your work from here," Anu again reminded her of her commitment.

Sunita nodded in agreement. She turned towards Karan, "You are a very courageous man, I can see that. You have given me hope. You have given me a reason to live. Perhaps, when we stop hating people across the border, we will learn to love. God bless you!" She hugged Karan and held on to him for more than a moment.

They all said their farewells and started their journey back to Delhi. The return journey was comparatively very quiet. Each one of them was either lost in his/her own thoughts or was busy with their phones.

Suddenly, Sumit exclaimed, "Wow! We have more than ten thousand shares and likes in a few hours!"

"What?" Karan did not follow and looked at him questioningly.

"Karan, I had published the videos of today's event on the internet. The response is very good. Of course, the likes and positive responses are from non-Pakistanis. There are many nasty comments too. But I am pretty amazed at how fast reactions have started to pour in. Very soon, our movement will become quite popular." Sumit could not contain his excitement, and it was obvious from his face that he was very thrilled.

"That's a good job, Sumit," Anu patted him on his back.

"Oh! This is when I have not even started to work on it. I have not boosted the page nor sponsored our post. I have not even started to reach out to the people," he said a little pompously.

"Then the credit should go to Karan's idea," Anu squeezed his shoulder.

"My friend is going to become famous," Vivek declared.

"Your friend is going to create history!" Anu corrected him with a smile.

Sumit's news had broken the lull in the conversation, and fresh excitement brewed in the air. They started discussing the way forward.

Just then, Anu got a call on her phone. One look at the screen, and her smile suddenly vanished and she became serious.

She disconnected the call, but it started ringing again.

She then received the call with a scowl on her face, "Why are you calling me?"

The person on the other side said something, and her reaction turned even more vehement.

"Even if I am admitted to a mental asylum, it is none of your concern. You continue the path of violence that you have chosen, and I walk down my chosen path. Don't bother me again. I just can't tolerate hearing your voice," she said as she disconnected the call again.

This time, the person did not call back.

No one said anything. They were all curious to know who that person was, but they did not ask.

After some moments of silence, Anu herself volunteered information

"The call was from my ex-boyfriend. We were dating a long time back when we were in college. Then we parted ways. He is an active member of 'Hindu Maha Morcha.' It is a group which believes that Hindus need to take up arms to safeguard their interest. He wanted to know if I had gone senile because I was talking about India and Pakistan's unity. He said that as if being a messenger of peace was not enough, I am also becoming a messenger of psychosis. That man! I hate him to the core!"

Vivek, who was sitting next to her, gave her hand a comforting squeeze.

"We will bump into many such people Anu, and we have to learn to deal with them," he said, and Karan too nodded in agreement.

"Don't you think it is a good sign that it has caught the interest of the Hindu Maha Morcha?" Asked Sumit. "Now the news will spread like wildfire. The more they talk about us, good or bad, the more people will come to know about us. The more people know about us, the chances of people joining our movement will also increase. I think we have set the ball rolling," he again had that pompous look on his face.

This time, no one responded as they were lost in their own thoughts as the car sped on the road, as if in a hurry to reach its destination.

NEW DELHI

It was a week after they reached Delhi that they met again, mainly to decide the future course of action.

Sumit had begun campaigning aggressively on social media, and their video had already garnered more than a million views from all over the world. Of course, there were many hateful comments, but many people had supported the idea too.

In Pakistan, however, this was getting more negative publicity than positive feedback. There were people who were saying that India wanted to invade Pakistan, and that this was just a ploy. One journalist also reported that it was the brainchild of Hindu Maha Morcha to attack Pakistan and make India and Pakistan a Hindu Nation!

All eight of them — Karan, Vivek, Anu, Sumit, Sudha, Manpreet, Iqbal, and Ramlal, met in the lawns of the India Gate.

Riyaz also joined them via video call. He was at Lahore, trying to garner support but without much success as yet.

They updated each other with the progress they had made at their own levels. They were all of the opinion that some concrete plan should be made because their movement had started to become a little popular now. There were many people who had joined their social pages, and many had shown interest in joining the physical movement.

One man from Punjab had written, "My great-grandfather died remembering his childhood days at Lahore, his school, his friends. His parents had been killed in the riots, but he had survived. He died with the scar of partition on his soul. I want to be a part of the movement that may unite the two countries after a hundred years."

There were numerous emotions that poured in from different parts of the world. Everyone had their own view or suggestion as to how it should be done. Indians wanted Pakistan to be merged in India, and Pakistanis wanted it the other way.

They decided to start a signature campaign online, and this responsibility was given to Sumit. They also decided to hold more public meetings and press conferences. Vivek and Iqbal volunteered themselves for this task.

Sudha was assigned the task of getting donations for the cause. The work was increasing, and as a result, the expenses were also mounting. Any cause, however great, needs funds to survive. They also opened an online registration form for registering themselves as volunteers for this movement for peace by the union of India and Pakistan.

Things were moving faster than they had expected, and they were gearing themselves to cope with the work that entailed. Looking at the overwhelming response they were getting from the public, they decided to hold the next public meeting in Delhi with all the new members. Thereafter, meetings trvould be held at different state capitals depending upon the number of members who enrolled.

They also decided to have a proper office from where they could operate. Vivek offered a flat he owned which was lying vacant in Lajpat Nagar. It would take a few days to get it cleaned and furnished, he said. They decided to meet at the new office in the coming weekend.

The way things were falling in place, one after the other, Karan was more and more convinced that all this was predestined. He was merely a puppet, and the strings were in the hands of someone who had orchestrated everything. He had a feeling that he was on the verge of a major transformation.

After the meeting ended, they went their own ways. Karan had some work so he had to go to South Extension market. He asked if anyone wanted something from there.

Anu said, "I don't want anything, but I don't mind doing some window shopping. It's been ages since I have gone to a proper market. As it is, I don't have my vehicle today. Can I come with you?" She asked.

"Yes, why not? I wanted to buy a pashmina shawl for Fiza. It will be a great help if you come along," he smiled at her, oblivious to the disenchanted look on Anu's face at the mention of Fiza's name.

They drove in the Delhi traffic, and it took them nearly an hour to reach their destination. As they were alighting from the car, Karan's phone rang. It was Fiza.

"Hi sweetheart, what's up?" He asked. "I am going to buy a small gift for you, and Anu is going to help me choose it," he said, again oblivious to the fact that Fiza did not sound very enthusiastic about it.

"Oh, you are not alone, are you? Call me when you are free," she said and disconnected the call.

Karan was taken aback by her abruptness.

"I think she did not like the fact that you are with me," Anu stated as a matter of fact.

"No, I think she wanted to speak to me about something and was not very happy when she could not," Karan was trying to mask his bewilderment.

"Why don't you call her and talk to her? Tell her that I got some urgent call and had to leave. She must have something important to share," Anu told Karan.

Karan was not sure about lying to Fiza, but he wanted to speak to her urgently and did not want to wait till Anu was gone. So, he moved away from Anu and called Fiza.

"Sweetheart, what's the matter?" He asked Fiza.

"No, she had to leave as she got some urgent call," Anu heard Karan say, though he was speaking softly.

Karan was quiet for some time with a serious look on his face as he tried to assimilate what was being said.

"I assure you Fiza that your name will not be dragged into this entire episode. I understand your need for privacy and that it would affect your aunt adversely. Rest assured, no one will know the name of the girl who is the protagonist of the entire story," he tried to be jovial about it.

As he continued his conversation with Fiza, he started walking further away from Anu, and she could not hear any more of what was being said.

He came back after a few minutes and smiled, "All is well! You girls have to be handled with care, and I love her so much that I can do anything for her."

Anu gave a feeble smile to his statement and said, "Fiza is a lucky girl."

She then looked at her watch and exclaimed, "I actually need to leave. I just remembered that I had promised my sister that I would take her out this evening." She waved at him and walked away to hail a cab.

Karan was left staring at her receding back.

"Women!" He said, and shrugged as he entered the market.

Anu was irritated at herself for feeling possessive about Karan. She had no right to feel this way. Then why had seen been jealous when Fiza had called, and why had she been upset when she had seen the change in his expression when he had been speaking to Fiza. There was a doting look on his face, and there was no doubt in her mind that he loved her very much. After all, all this would not have started if he was not serious about Fiza.

Though Anu had said that she had some urgent meeting, it was not true. She suddenly felt very low and wanted to be alone.

The call from Sooraj the other day, when they were returning from Chhabua village, had disturbed her. It was after ages that she had heard his voice. Why did he have to call her when she had learnt to live without him? Listening to his voice had opened the wounds that she thought were healed.

Anu went to her room and lay down on the bed. The pink bedspread with blue cushions always lifted her mood as this was her most favorite buy from the Jaipur Crafts Mela. Today, even this did not cheer her up.

She got up and opened her laptop. There was a folder that she had not opened for years. This folder had memories she wanted to forget. She had thought that by locking away all the photographs in a folder, she would perhaps be able to lock away his memories. She had succeeded to some extent. She was happy with her life and all that she had achieved. It was just that listening to his voice after years had rattled her. The fact that she could see how much Karan loved Fiza did not help matters.

She was capable of loving with no holds barred, but she had not met anyone who deserved her love.

She used to think that she had met that special person when she met Sooraj. She had loved him deeply and intensely, but he turned out to be like the others. He did not value her love. They had been a couple in JNU, always hanging out together. She loved him, and she made no secret about that fact. He loved her too, but did not want a commitment. Like a typical man, he wanted to keep his options open. After nearly a year of hanging together, he had dumped her for another girl. God! How she had hated that girl, Sakshi! She was nothing great to look at and had neither beauty nor brains. What Sooraj had seen in her, she could never understand. He had married Sakshi after two years.

Anu wanted someone in her life who would always make her a priority, someone who would do anything for her, the way Karan was ready to embark on a path untrodden and unknown for Fiza.

Well, her mission in life was to bring love and peace on the planet, to make this world a better place to live in. If she ever married anyone and became a mother, she would not want to bring her child into a world that was vandalized by terrorists, a world where one's religion was more important than humanity, a world where people lived in fear — fear that tomorrow might never come.

Anu closed her laptop and looked outside the window. The sun was sliding behind the Qutub Minar. From her room, she had a clear view of the magnificent monument. She loved to see the setting sun and the way all the leaves on the trees turned red like a blushing bride.

She took out the medicine box and popped a pill. Then, she went to the kitchen and made a cup of coffee for herself. At times like these, when she was in a pensive mood, she liked to sit on the rocking chair in her balcony with a cup of coffee and look at the setting sun. The way the sky bids farewell to the sun only to welcome the moon in some time, likewise in our lives, people leave only so that new people can come in. In her case, instead of a person, a cause and a purpose had come into her life.

'Life has been good,' Anu thought to herself. From being a small-town girl to earning a name for herself in her field, she had come a long way. She closed her eyes and rested her head on the cushion. With the coffee in her right hand, she occasionally lifted her head to take sips of the hot beverage. A gentle breeze softly caressed her cheeks. The air against her skin felt like the soft kisses of a lover. She felt calm.

'I have done well for myself. I have come a long way, and I have a long way to go! Nothing and no one will stop me from achieving my goals. Let all the Soorajs of the world try!' She thought to herself as she opened her eyes to catch the last glimpse of the red ball of fire sliding behind the tall frame of the Minar.

ISLAMABAD, PAKISTAN

The streets where he had grown up had now changed beyond recognition. The place where they used to play football had been converted into a multi-level parking. A new mall had come up where there used to be a small local market. Riyaz wondered what had happened to Jamaal Miyan who used to sell meat in the local shop. It was Riyaz's responsibility to get fresh meat from the shop every day, and Jamaal Miyan would always give him the best of the lot. He would ask him about his studies and would also tell him how he wanted his sons to settle abroad instead of looking to make a career in Islamabad.

"Living in Islamabad is like living on the tip of a volcano," he would say. "Every day there are bomb blasts in some part of the city or the other. It has become so common that we have accepted it as part of our lives."

"*Chhote Miyan, aap bhi chale jao bahar, zinda to rahoge,*" he would advise him, and tell him to go to Dubai. Riyaz did take Jamaal Miya's advice, but he did not go to Dubai. He went to London instead.

He always wanted to come back to his country, his motherland. He loved London, but it was not home! There was no place where people did not look at him with suspicion. He, with his beard and Asian looks faced hidden hostility at most of the places. At some places, natives were downright rude and insulting! It made his blood boil, but he controlled himself. His own country was no better. There were bomb blasts every day along with many clashes between different communities like Shia and Sunni. 'Some things never change,' he thought sadly.

Riyaz had landed in Islamabad just the day before. When Karan had left London to convince his father, Riyaz had not thought much about it. Then, a few days back, he had called from Delhi and shared with him the idea of uniting India and Pakistan.

Riyaz had not laughed at this idea, because he always felt that had the British not played their divide-and-rule policy, India would have been a country to reckon with, a superpower by now! For there was something that the East had which the West did not. The East had the wealth of wisdom which was handed over to them as a legacy from their ancestors. After the partition, the strength got divided, and just as the British had conspired, the two new countries got busy fighting each other soon after.

'If we had not been fighting wars all these years, we would have definitely developed at a faster rate. The idea of uniting India and Pakistan was awesome,' he thought, 'though not practical or likely to happen, at least not in the near future.' But he was still interested in this idea for two reasons. Firstly, the foundation for a way of thinking would be laid. Who knew, perhaps his grandchildren would live in a united India and Pakistan. Secondly, if not union, at least peace could be restored between the two countries if the youth of both the nations came together to demand it. That is what he wanted — peace in his motherland.

His annual visit to Islamabad was due anyway. So he had come. He wanted to see what could be done here, and if things started to move, perhaps he would extend his stay.

Riyaz had been raised by his mother alone as his father had left her for his second wife. His mother was from Kashmir in India, but she did not go back to her home after the separation. His father had not divorced her as his community rules permitted more than one wife, but people generally did not have more than one wife. His mother often spoke about her village in Kashmir and would always tell him that people across both sides of the border are good at heart. It's only that they are taught to consider each other as enemies.

Riyaz had never been to his mother's native village because when he was young, his father did not allow it, and later, when his father had walked away from them, his mother's parents were no longer alive, and as she had made Pakistan her home, she stopped visiting her native village.

"It is of no use to open old wounds," she would say. Riyaz wanted to visit his Indian grandparents' village once in his lifetime.

When Riyaz shared Karan's idea of uniting India and Pakistan with his mother, she listened to it very seriously. Then with a somber face, she asked, "Is your friend seeing a doctor?"

Riyaz was taken aback at the question.

"*Ammi,* why are you saying this?" He asked.

"Anyone who can even think of such a thing can only be insane or an idealist daydreamer. In both cases, it requires medical attention," she said with a straight face.

"You don't have to be sarcastic," he said.

"I am not being sarcastic; I am just stating this as a matter of fact. I know how difficult it was for me to settle in this country after marriage. Even though I did my best, and I literally gave up my country and my identity, even then the tag of being born an 'Indian' has never left me. I could never be good enough for the people here. Even marrying a girl from Pakistan will be difficult for him, and more so for her. He should forget his daydream of uniting India and Pakistan for the best."

'My mother is carrying many scars from her past,' Riyaz thought. He knew it had been very difficult for her, so he kept quiet and did not probe further.

Today, he had a hearty breakfast of his favorite dish, *churi*, and went to meet his college friends. He had a long list of activities that needed to be done. Whatever his mother might say, he had been stung by the contagious spark in Karan's voice, and as he had known him for a long time now, he knew that once Karan became obsessed with something, he would not rest until that task was finished. Possible, impossible, logical, illogical, a vision, or a pipe dream, he did not know what it was, but he knew that Karan was a leader that he would like to follow. Wherever it took them, he knew it would be a place worth going!

NEW DELHI

Days were slipping into weeks and weeks were transforming into months. Time was flying as if it had grown wings! It had already been three months since Karan came to India. His leave period had expired, and he had to send his resignation because he could not go back. He did not want to continue with the job anyway.

He sometimes felt as if he was in the middle of a river and the currents were carrying him forward. He had stopped trying to swim and was going with the flow. Things were happening one after the other. What he had never imagined was coming true.

When he had come to India, his sole motive was to convince his father to give his blessings for his marriage with Fiza. He had known it would be a difficult task, but not even in his dreams had he imagined the direction in which the events would progress.

An idea that seemed ridiculous in the beginning was now being discussed in public and social media. Yes, they had created quite a stir! After the initial meeting at Chhabua, where this idea was implanted in people's minds for the first time, there had been a few more public meetings. The social media campaigning was also going on in full swing. People had started responding, and with the kind of reactions they were getting, to say that they had put their hands in the hornet's nest would be an understatement.

While there were many people who mocked them and thought that they were crazy, many were calling them agents of Pakistan. They were accused of trying to bring disharmony by inciting volatile sentiments! Disharmony? They were talking of peace! Good or bad, the best part was that they were getting noticed, and they were getting a lot of publicity.

Last month, Karan had been called for many video interviews and three interviews with different television channels. Whereas most interviewers were interested in bringing out the unique thought process that Karan was trying to convey, the TV channel, '*Aaj ki awaaz*' seemed to be hell bent on projecting Karan as an agent of Pakistan, and it almost seemed like they had a preset agenda against him and his idea. Karan normally never reacted to the baits people threw at him to rile him up, but this time, he lost his cool when the interviewer would not let him speak at all and spoke nonstop about his opinions and accusations. Karan left the room in anger, and this was in turn used by the channel to further tarnish his image.

Whenever Karan would talk about how this all started, one obvious question was, who was the girl? People wanted to give a name and a face to the girl who was instrumental in starting something so unique and path-breaking.

Karan would only smile and keep quiet. He was bound by his promise to Fiza. Come what may, he could not disclose her identity to the public. He had also given strict instructions to his own group not to disclose her identity to anyone. He had told her name only to a few people. Anu, of course, had seen Fiza and even spoken to her, but even she did not know where she worked or what her full name was.

Karan missed Fiza a lot. In fact, in the beginning, he used to talk to her many times a day. Lately, of course, he was getting caught up in the whirlwind of activities and the calls were becoming less frequent. Many times when she called, he was with people and was not able to talk to her.

"Karan, I feel you are sometimes forgetting the original motive of why all this was started. I fear that you might win Pakistan but lose me," she had laughed over the phone yesterday, trying to pull his leg. Even though it was said in jest, it had hurt Karan.

"Fiza, I can't imagine a life without you. Even though my life seems to be moving at the pace of a jet plane, believe me, you are the first thought on my mind when I wake up and the last one when I go to sleep. Often when I feel dejected or low, I only have to think of you and my vigor gets renewed. You are my goal, you are my destination, but unfortunately, the path is so behest with hardships that I am trying to find my way. Sometimes, I feel like a prince who is riding on his horse in a dense jungle with his sword, cutting through the forest and slaying demons to reach his princess, who has been sleeping peacefully in the castle for years."

Fiza laughed again at his metaphor. Her laughter was music to his ears. How she ruled over his heart! He sometimes wondered about love. With time, everything changes — people, technology and value systems. What remain unchanged are human emotions. Love still plays on the heartstrings with the same frequency it did hundreds of years ago. Love is such an intense emotion that it has changed the course of history many a time. Love, if made a strength, had the power to move mountains, and if made a weakness could destroy generations!

Karan smiled at his thoughts. He was becoming a thinker, a philosopher!

Today, after a long time, he could devote some time for himself. After the morning meeting with a group of students from a technical institute in Noida, he had to go to Delhi University's north campus for another meeting with a college union. This got cancelled at the last minute. He decided to go back to his house and gather his thoughts. He sometimes got this feeling that his own life was not in his control any more. This was a disturbing thought. He wanted to sit and contemplate how he could reach his goal faster. He wanted his father to look at the efforts he was making. He wanted to bring some peace between the two countries so that his father would appreciate his sincerity and agree to give his blessings.

He had not spent any time with his family. He felt guilty about that too. He sometimes thought about how selflessly his uncle had raised him like his own son. He, on the other hand, had not only given him a tough time growing up, but even now, he somehow always took his love and affection for granted. Uncle was more of a friend than a father figure. Even aunty never made him feel that he was not her own son. He suddenly felt like a heel for being so selfish.

On his way home, he got some *samosas* and *pyaz ki kachori* packed from a very old and famous shop in Chandni Chowk. His father and uncle loved samosas, and aunty was a big fan of onion *kachoris*.

They were surprised to see him so early during the day. Aunty was busy reading a book and uncle was sitting on the sofa. He looked worried.

"Uncle, what's the matter? You are not looking your normal self." Karan asked, sitting next to him on the sofa.

"*Bhaiyya* is not feeling well," he told him, looking straight into his eyes. Why did he feel that he was accusing him?

No, it's nothing like that. Guilty minds are always suspicious, he thought, feeling guiltier about his behavior.

"What happened to papa? Where is he?" He asked.

"He is resting. His blood pressure climbed higher than normal," he replied, this time averting his eyes.

Karan had a feeling that there was more to it. Uncle was never so guarded with his words.

"Uncle, you are hiding something from me. Tell me please, what happened? How did his blood pressure suddenly shoot up?" Karan asked, but he had a feeling that he knew what was coming.

"Since you want to know, I will tell you, even though *bhaiyya* forbade me to do so. For the last couple of months, we have been receiving threat calls on the phone, which I am sure you must also be receiving. Last week, there was a reporter at our house. He got entry by posing as a distant relative, but we soon came to know his real motive. He was insisting on holding an interview with your father, which we refused to entertain. When he still persisted with his pestering, *bhaiyya* lost his cool and literally pushed him out of the house.

"Today, by chance, we saw an article on his news channel website where they have accused your father of harboring an anti-national. The article is titled 'War hero harbors an antinational! Blood is thicker than water!' You better read it yourself. He was very agitated after reading it and also went to their office. I don't know what happened there, but he came back a little while ago looking very flustered and distressed. We checked his blood pressure, and it was very high. So, I talked to our doctor and gave him the medicine."

Uncle looked relieved after sharing the incident with Karan, as if a weight had suddenly lifted off of his chest.

Karan kept staring at his face for a long time. When he had got into all this, he knew he would have to face rough weather. What he had not bargained for was that his family would be made a scapegoat too.

He could handle goons like these, but he did not expect his family to do so. In his college days, during elections and at other times, any such challenge would make his resolve to pursue the matter even stronger. But then, his family was never made a target.

He looked at his aunt who had been sitting quietly all through the discussion. She gestured him to come to her. He went and sat down on the floor near her, resting his head on her lap.

"*Chachi,* what should I do? All this is happening because of me," he said. His voice was muffled in the pleats of her *saree* as she gently stroked his head, running her fingers through his hair.

"Karan, do you remember that incident when you were in class five and a senior boy used to bully you? One day you came home crying and told me that you did not want to go to school. You also requested your uncle to go and talk to the boy. Your uncle told you that you need to learn to fight your own battles, and I told you to never give in to the bullies. They feed on our fears. The only way to defeat them is by being courageous. I want to give you the same advice today as well.

This is just the beginning of your struggle. The path ahead is going to be difficult. You have to draw strength from your purpose. Your goal should radiate its bright light upon your path so as to alleviate the darkness," she said in a calm and soothing voice as her fingers kept stroking his hair.

 "We also know you have a beautiful prize waiting for you at the end of the dark road," she laughed as she said this and bent down to plant a kiss on Karan's forehead.

Karan felt his eyes getting moist, and he wiped them using the corner of her *pallu*.

"Now go and meet your father. I am sure he must be awake by now," she nudged him, and he got up went to his father's bedroom.

"Papa, are you awake?" He asked softly.

'Yes, come in," came the reply.

"*Chacha ji* told me what happened. I am sorry," Karan sat down on the sofa.

"You are sorry? Are you sorry that you took up my challenge? Are you sorry about wanting to marry that Pakistani girl?" His father was quick to ask.

"No. No, I am sorry that all this happened. I am sorry that because of me you have to suffer indignities and insult."

"Insult? Indignity? Beta, you don't know the meaning of these words. Just a nitwit calling me a traitor's father isn't going to break me. Years ago, the enemies had tried all the tricks in the book, but they could not torture me enough to break my spirit. That joker who had to use tricks to get into my house, you think he or people like him will scare me? I am sure you know your father enough to not worry about me.

At the same time, if you are becoming weak at such intimidations, if you are stumbling at the first roadblock that comes your way, then I can only say that you cannot be my son," his father said, looking him in the eyes, as if daring him to say something.

'A military man will not change in his lifetime. The pride, the self-respect, the courage, the valor gets ingrained in their system from the day they don the khaki!' Karan thought.

Yet again, Karan felt proud of his father. He himself was indeed very daring, headstrong, and strong-willed, just like his father. But this time, for the first time in his life, he wondered if he had bitten off more than he could chew.

Sooraj had received the call about the meeting only an hour back. This meeting had been convened on a short notice. Not all the members were present. Prof Tyagi had called only a few selected members of the Hindu Maha Morcha. This was his inner circle, in which he kept only those people whom he trusted impeccably.

He had convened the meeting at his residence in Greater Kailash–II. His wife, a genial lady, was there in the room with them when Sooraj reached. She supervised the serving of tea and homemade *pakoras* to all his guests. After the tea and snacks, she asked the guests if they wanted anything else. When they assured her that they did not, she excused herself from the room and left quietly, closing the door behind her.

Prof Tyagi looked at her receding back, and when the door was firmly closed, he cleared his throat to speak.

"Friends, this sudden meeting has been called to alert ourselves about a threat that is looming over our heads these days. You all must have heard of Karan Thakur by now," he paused for effect, looking at all the faces around him who nodded in agreement.

"We initially thought he was a lunatic, a hare-brained person who got this outrageous idea of uniting India and Pakistan. Then we came to know that he is a very intelligent person who has come here with a proper plan. We found that in his college days he was very popular and was offered a place in the youth wing of almost all political parties, which he declined. In his youth, perhaps, he was not politically inclined. Things have now changed it seems, but we don't know for sure. Though he claims that he is doing this for some Pakistani girl whom he wants to marry, he could have married her anyway without creating all this mayhem.

Whatever his motive might be, it is certain that he is creating quite a stir. People here and even across the border are noticing him. This is bad news for us," Prof Tyagi again took that long melodramatic pause.

"But how can he be a threat to us? He can never achieve what he wants to achieve. We all know this," the oldest of the group, Mr Karmakar interrupted him, taking advantage of the pause.

Prof Tyagi looked at him and then he looked at the others, paused for another long moment, perhaps trying to build up curiosity and then said, "An enemy who is intelligent, detached, strong-willed and fearless is an enemy you should watch out for. This boy has all these traits."

This time, it was Sooraj who asked in a very reverent tone, "Sir, to tackle him, we should understand clearly all the aspects in which he can be a threat to us. I would request you to please tell us about it."

Prof Tyagi smiled at Sooraj. He liked him. He had himself inducted Sooraj into the Morcha years ago. So Sooraj was in a way his protégé.

"Sooraj," he said, "what we have been fighting for, is granting majority status to the Hindus in our own country. Hindustan is for Hindus, but look at the irony, we are fighting for our rights. The minority today is well off and growing exponentially." He looked at Sooraj and perhaps, reading the exasperation on his face, he nodded his head as if getting the cue for what to say next. "I know I am digressing. You have to pardon me; it's a very sensitive topic for me. Coming to your question now, I think he is a threat because this man is talking about love and peace. His intentions might or might not be political, but he will be approached by our rivals very soon and they will use him for their political gains.

"We don't want the other party to come to power. All the work that we have done till now will go down the drain. If they use this person, there are chances that they will get the votes of many misguided youths. The youth of today is fed up with the violence, and rightly so, but what they don't understand is that the only way to end this violence is to teach people their place. There will be peace and harmony only if there is fear."

Prof. Tyagi paused again and looked around the room.

Mr. Prasad, who was another senior member, came to his support. "Yes, I agree that we have to deal with him very cautiously. The way his popularity is growing, it is not good for our cause."

"What do you suggest we do?" Asked Mr. Karnakar again.

"Well, we should tell him to back off! If he wants to unite India and Pakistan or even wants peace, let him go to Pakistan and preach!" Sooraj was back to his usual self.

"Always impatient!" Prof. Tyagi chided him affectionately. "But this is what I like about him," he addressed the meeting again, giving his famous pause.

"Everything is either black or white for him. Once he decides someone is an enemy, there is no turning back," he paused again.

"Do you agree that this Karan is our enemy," he said with mock seriousness, looking at Sooraj.

Sooraj smiled, "Yes sir, now I understand why he needs to be stopped. Leave him to me. I will take care of it."

"One more thing. It is important that the points discussed in today's meeting remain only in our minds and are not recorded or communicated in any written form. Let it be amongst us only. There is no need to make others panic. We should be on our guard, that's it. Now, Sooraj will take care of this, umm, 'problem'," Prof. Tyagi paused again while the others looked at him, waiting for him to complete the sentence. "I am relieved," he said.

PRIME MINISTER'S OFFICE
SOUTH BLOCK, RAISINA HILLS, NEW DELHI

The big clock on the wall showed the time as 9 p.m. The man at the table glanced at the clock again. Certain things don't change. They stand more for sentimental or traditional value than for any real worth. This big wall clock was one such thing. It was more out of habit that he looked at the clock.

It was not unusual for Madam Prime Minister to work this late. He was used to this. But today was special. It was the 16th birthday of his eldest daughter, and he wanted to go home. They had planned a surprise party for her, and he had hoped to be home by 6. The Prime Minister was in a personal meeting and was going to leave the office by 6. Unfortunately, the meeting was cancelled, and she did not go. He also got stuck with her.

There was a call on his personal number. It was his daughter. He took the call and she started blowing kisses at him.

"Dad, thank you for this surprise party. When are you coming home? This year I am not cutting the cake without you," she said.

Her voice resonated in the big hall. He immediately switched his phone into audio mode and held the receiver next to his ear.

"Darling, I will be late. Madam is still in her office, and I can't come till she grants me leave for the day. I am sorry, honey," he said in a muffled voice and just then the intercom flashed.

"Sorry, I have to go, She is calling," he spoke softly on the mouthpiece and disconnected the call.

He went to her room and knocked softly, silently praying that she wouldn't start a discussion on some topic tonight.

"Come in," she said.

 Isn't it your daughter's birthday today?" She asked.

"Yes, ma'am. She has turned sixteen today."

"Then what are you doing at the office? Go home."

"Yes ma'am," he said as he felt relief wash over him as he turned around to leave.

"Just a moment, Kamal. Who is this 'Karan Thakur'?" She asked casually. "He is making headlines these days."

"Yes ma'am, he is. From what I have heard, he lives in London and wants to marry a Pakistani girl. His father was a survivor in the war of 2028 and was also awarded the Param Vir Chakra for his valor. This unique demand was his condition for giving his approval to this marriage; obviously, this demand was made to desist him from marrying her, and hence, this strange idea. I have already asked my people to prepare a detailed dossier on him and will submit it to you tomorrow."

"Good! Elections are near. We can't take a chance."

"Yes ma'am," he replied as he was aware of the gravity of the situation. Whenever public sentiments are involved in any issue, one is never really sure in which direction the tide will turn.

"Now leave and buy a gift for your daughter from my side," the prime minister said, taking out a gift envelope from her purse and giving it to him.

Kamal thanked her. He had worked with many ministers, mostly male but some female. One major difference he noticed in their work was that women always somehow remembered the small niceties of life that made life so beautiful.

Putting the envelope in his pocket, Kamal went out of the door, gently closing it behind him, and left the lady in the room toiling hard to build a better future for the nation.

NEW DELHI

Ekta Party had called for a monthly meeting to review the progress of the work which the party workers had been doing. Top party workers from all over the North Indian states were present today. On the stage stood the senior leaders who were already done giving their motivational speeches to get the fire burning in the hearts of the workers. Elections were not very far off, and the public sentiment was tilting towards them because the general public was sick of the wars and bombings. They wanted peace and unity. Even then, one could never be sure about such matters. They had to keep toiling hard to garner public support for the party.

It was now the turn of the party workers to speak if they had something important to share. One by one, they came on the stage and voiced their opinions.

Mr Roshan Sharma was feeling bored on the stage. Not a single party worker had come up with any good idea. 'What is happening to the youth these days?' He thought. They were too busy with their phones and games to worry about the future. Not that he was old; he was in his late forties. The new generation was getting more and more selfish with time. He was now getting restless. He wanted to leave the meeting on the pretense of having some urgent work, but just then, the words of the current speaker caught his attention.

This party worker was in his early twenties with tall, fair, curly hair, broad forehead, and a sharp nose. 'He should try his hand at the movies,' was Roshan's first thought.

The way he was speaking was also very impressive, but the content was what caught his attention.

"This is the time when we need to build upon the public sentiments, which are in our favour. We need to speak the language they are speaking; we need to feel the pain they are feeling; we need to dream the dreams they are dreaming," he continued. This boy was undoubtedly a good speaker.

"Today, we have a new hero among the masses. Karan Thakur has suddenly come into the limelight and became very famous. Do you know why? Because he does not talk of war, he does not talk of hate, and he does not talk of teaching anyone a lesson. He is talking of love, he is talking of peace, and he is talking of unity, unity between India and Pakistan. Of course, the dream that he is showing people is absurd, but that is not the point. The point is that he has given people something that they have always wanted – hope. Hope for a better future where there is no war. Hope for a day when the youth who join the army are not considered as sacrificial lambs. Hope for a day when we will again talk of brotherhood and not brutality."

"People are listening to him, many to ridicule and scoff, but they are listening. I think that before anyone gets to him and uses him as their pawn, we should approach him and tell him that we are the right people to fulfill his dreams. His dreams, if moderated properly, will sync with our own agenda. Our party is also for peace and brotherhood. Let's get him in our fold. This will definitely boost our public image."

Roshan and other senior leaders on stage were listening to him attentively. Some of them had heard of Karan Thakur, and they were nodding their heads in agreement.

Roshan interrupted him and asked, "What's your name, young chap? Sorry, I did not get it."

"Sandy, sir."

"Sandy, contact him today and fix up his meeting with me. Let me screen him first, and then we will take it further," he said.

"Yes sir, I will do that," Sandy said, looking mighty pleased with himself for getting the attention of one of the most dynamic leaders of the party.

Roshan decided to excuse himself from the meeting, but he was happy that he had not missed what this 'Sandy' had to say. Somehow, he had a feeling that this Karan would play an important role in the larger scheme of things.

What was politics but a game of chess? Everything depended on who made well-planned moves to outthink the opponent. If the strategy is right, even a pawn can slay a king!

NEWHAM, LONDON

Fiza was feeling very low. She was sitting at her desk, staring at the list of official calls she had to make. She also had a few important client meetings but did not feel like doing anything. The work was the same. This feeling had nothing to do with the work, the same old clients, and the same old business targets. Nothing much had changed in her work life, but her work did not excite her anymore.

This was something which had never happened to her before. She had always loved her work. Whatever blues she might be feeling, they would all disappear once she was at her workstation. Rather than having Monday morning blues, she rather had Friday evening blues! But after she met Karan, this had changed too.

She looked forward to Fridays, and they used to rock the weekend together; going to parties, movies, gaming zones or simply chilling at home over drinks and conversation. They would lie on the bed, make love and talk for hours, leaving it only when they were hungry.

After he left, there was a vacuum in her life. She had never missed anyone as much as she missed him. But then, no one had ever come this close!

Today was Friday. She was dreading the two long days ahead. Even if she did not enjoy working, at least she was with people and not alone. The weekend would find her in the company of Felicia, eating, sleeping and counting the hours till Monday. The only high point of the weekend would be the long video chat with Karan.

Karan had lately become very busy, and most of the time, he was with people. They could only communicate through audio calls. It was really frustrating sometimes. She missed his face, his laugh, his touch, his care and his warmth. London became cold after he left.

Is this what love does to people? Does it make them useless? Karan had spoiled her, and now she did not want anyone else's company.

'Enough!' She chided herself. 'I will not sit and sulk like a lovelorn teenager. Let me go and hang out with my friends.'

She called up Rhonda. Rhonda was an obvious choice because she had met Karan. She and her boyfriend had gone on double dates with them many times. She was genuinely fond of Karan and kept on reminding Fiza that she should never let him go. God has stopped making specimens like Karan, she would often joke.

Even when he is not here, I want to talk to those people who will talk about him, Fiza thought to herself.

Rhonda agreed to meet her in the evening. She suggested that they meet for dinner at the Indian restaurant, the Gymkhana. This is where they had had their first date and also where he had proposed to her. 'Why was everything about him? Did he also miss her the way she missed him?' She did not feel so.

The brain is a funny thing. It needs something to be mad about. For Fiza's brain, it was her relationship with Karan; for him, the focus had slightly shifted, and it seemed his insanity was now about his purpose. He would often remind her that everything he was doing was for her. She did not think so. It was he who had been adamant to get married and that too after taking the blessings of his father! She did not mind a live-in relationship.

Slowly, things were changing. It was no longer about his father. It was about a dream that he saw, a purpose that his heart found, an objective that was becoming an obsession!

Fiza went home and dressed in a *churidar kurta*. This was a beautiful *anarkali kurta* in pastel blue with intricate *zardozi* work. It was a gift from Karan.

Letting her hair loose, she picked up a *potli bag* to complete her Indian ensemble. She looked at the mirror in front of her. She was looking good and she knew it. She wanted Karan to see her. She dialed his number. He must be sleeping. It was 8 p.m. in London, and so, it must be well past midnight in Delhi, she thought. She hesitated for a moment, and then dialed his number.

He was awake. He picked up her call immediately, but he switched to audio mode. He was in the office with other team members.

"Fiza, guess what? People have started to notice me and are talking about my mission!" Karan sounded like a schoolboy who had received a new video game.

"Why are you working this late? I wanted to talk to you," she asked.

"Oh, the meeting was in the evening but it got dragged till the night. Then we ordered for food in the office itself. We just finished dinner," he replied, with the excitement still in his voice.

In his excitement, he failed to notice the disappointment in her voice.

Fiza, on the other hand, was quick to revert to her usual chirpy self.

"Ok then, we will catch up later," she said, and blew a kiss as she disconnected the phone.

She looked at the mirror again but she couldn't see anything. Everything was a blur. God! Was she in tears?

No! It can't be! She did not remember the last time that she had cried! She was tough, really tough. She would laugh at the sentimental movies when her friends would all be teary-eyed. Tears were for weaklings, and she was certainly not weak!

She sat down on the sofa! This was getting out of control. She needed to take control. Love was turning her into someone she never thought she would become. Love was making her vulnerable and soft, and she did not like it! Not one bit!

Wiping her tears with the corner of her hand, she picked up the *potli* bag once again and went out into the night, perhaps searching for the self that she had lost when she found love!

NEW DELHI

Karan woke up with a headache. He had not slept peacefully the previous night. The meeting with the team in their office had continued till late at night.

Everyone had many stories to share and also a lot of ideas about how to take things forward. Sometimes, the mood was very upbeat, but at other times, they would wonder where they all were heading.

It was Karan and Anu who would always keep the others motivated by giving pep talks and telling them that they would be the catalysts in a change, which perhaps, would be the biggest change after the partition. From this perspective, it did seem like they were going down in history or at least being a part of history.

The previous night, they all had ordered pizza and had just finished their dinner when Fiza had called up. In the mayhem that was prevailing in the room, he could not talk to her. He intended to do that today, but before that he needed to do something about the headache. It was splitting his head into two.

Karan was still on the bed, and without opening his eyes, he looked for the medicine in the bedside drawer. When he found the bottle of blue pills, he took out one and gulped it down with water.

He hit the pillow again, waiting for the headache to subside. It was then that his phone rang. Thinking that it would be Fiza, he quickly answered it. Immediately, he realized his folly when he saw that it was some unknown person who was calling. He quickly switched to speaker mode.

"Good morning, who am I talking to?'" He asked, cursing himself for taking the call without checking who was calling.

"Is it Karan Thakur?" The person asked. It must be someone from some news channel wanting to take his interview, he thought.

These days, there was a lot of competition amongst the channels, and they all were on their toes to cover any masala news in the market. "Yes, I am Karan Thakur. How can I help you? Who am I speaking with?" He repeated again.

 "You don't know me. My name is Sandy. Well, it is Sundar, but everyone calls me Sandy," he replied.

The headache was getting worse, and this Sandy was certainly contributing to it.

"Look, if it is about an interview, can we talk about it later, Sandy?" Karan asked.

"No, it's not about any interview. I am a party worker for Ekta Party. We are very impressed with the work you are doing. There are many common grounds in your vision and our manifesto." Sandy sounded as if he was not sure how to approach the subject.

Karan was now all ears! Ekta Party was one of the largest parties in the country, and although they were not in power at the center, they were in power in many of the states.

"Look, Sandy, I think you got some wrong information. I do not have a political agenda and neither do I have any interest in politics. I am just a person with some dreams which many people are calling ludicrous. I am taking the help of like-minded people who have no affiliation with any political parties. I think I will not be able to help you at all," Karan said patiently and was about to hang up.

"Don't hang up, please! Can we just meet for coffee somewhere? I am not asking anything from you. Just hear me out please," he almost pleaded.

Karan did not have the heart to turn him down. "Okay, meet me at Oxford store, Connaught Place, in the evening."

He had promised to take his aunt out for shopping that day. He had been promising her for a long time. 'So I might as well meet him and get him off my back,' he thought.

After disconnecting the phone, he thought of calling Fiza but the headache was not getting any better. So, he went back to sleep.

Karan had almost dozed off when the phone rang again. He half opened his eyes this time to see that it was a call from Fiza. The remnants of the headache were still there, and he was feeling drowsy. In spite of that he took the video call. She was sitting on her bed, and the crumpled sheets told the tale of a restless night. The eyes looked heavy as if she had been crying. She still had the makeup from the previous night on her face.

"What happened, sweetheart? You are not looking well," he asked out of concern.

"You expect a girl to look glamorous at 6 a.m. in the morning?" She quipped.

'She certainly is not in a good mood today,' he thought. "You look glamorous at any time of the day or night, but right now, you are looking different, tired and listless. Are you all right?" He could not shrug off the uneasy feeling that was growing in his heart.

"No, I am not all right!" she retorted, her voice rising involuntarily. "Before I met you, I was fine and was enjoying my work and my social life. Ever since I met you, nothing else gives me happiness except being with you. I have become addicted to you, Karan, and I do not like it one bit." Karan was aghast to see tears streaming down her face.

So, she had been crying, he thought. "Baby, it's the same for me. I have also become addicted to you. I need you, and I am doing all this for us," he spoke very slowly as if wanting every word to seep into her mind, washing away all the doubts that she had.

"No, Karan. It's not the same with you. You are with your friends and family. You are so busy with your, eh…mission, that you barely have time to talk to me. I am not sure whether it is about us anymore." She finally managed to say what had been bothering her for some time now.

"Fiza, I know I have become very busy lately. Even then, you are always my topmost priority. Believe me, you might be segregating this mission from us, but for me, this mission is about us. It has always been about us. I will be honest with you; it has become much bigger than what I had imagined initially. When I had started talking about unity and peace, I had no idea I would be triggering such strong emotions in people. Yes, things sometimes feel out of hand, but please believe me Fiza, for me, everything is about you." He wished that there was some machine which would show to her the kind of feelings he had for her. Unfortunately, however much science advanced, it could never outdo the Almighty.

"Fiza, do you know, a member from the Ekta Party called up saying he wants to meet me," Karan could not mask the excitement in his voice.

"Oh, it's getting too political, Karan. I don't like it anymore. Very soon, some snoopy journalist will find out about me, and my *khala*'s name will get dragged into it." Fiza suddenly became very alert.

"Don't panic! Nothing like that is going to happen. They are trying to gain political mileage out of my mission and the public sentiments that it has aroused. Once they meet me, they will understand my resolve and stop bothering me."

"Karan, Just remember one thing, I love you very much, and I don't want to lose you because of someone's political agenda. What you started to bring us together, should not become the reason for our separation," she said, and blew a kiss at him before disconnecting the call.

Karan was left staring at the blank screen of the phone. What was happening? Was he gaining control of the external things but losing control of his own life?

Sooraj kept staring at his phone, not being able to make up his mind whether to call her or not. The last time he had called Anu, they had ended up fighting. He was in no mood for a fight nor did he want to annoy her. Anu had been a very good friend in his college days. In fact, she had been more than a friend.

He remembered the first time that he had seen her. He had gone to the college reception for some work. As he was parking his bike outside the room, he noticed her sitting on the bench outside the reception, looking hassled and annoyed. She had cropped her hair in a boyish way and had colored it dark pink. She was wearing a big hoop in one ear and a stud in the other; pink fluorescent sunglasses were perched on her nose. Whether she was pretty or not, he could not decide, but she was definitely not a person you could ignore!

She was fiddling with a single stiletto in her hand. The heel appeared to be broken. He went and asked her, "Can I help you?"

She looked up at him and was about to say no when she noticed his bike.

"Yes, you can," she said. "The heel of my footwear is broken, and I need to go to the market to get it repaired. Can you give me a lift till the market?" She said, pointing at the bike.

"Or better still, I think I will go and change into my sandals. Can you drop me home and wait for a moment while I change my footwear?" She smiled at him and took off her glasses.

She was not pretty, he noticed. Her nose was too big and her eyes were small and deep-set. She had a lovely smile though! And he also noticed that her face did not have any makeup. Not even *kajal*. Nude face with funky hair and florescent sunglasses, she was certainly someone you would notice twice!

"Why not? Give me two minutes," he said.

He got to know that she had just enrolled for the Political Science honors course, and this was her first day. They had gone to her paying guest accommodation near the college that day for Anu to change into her sandals. After that, he frequented that place very often. They became very good friends, and he enjoyed her company.

It was after a few months that they became intimate. Sex with her was great, and they both enjoyed it. They were more like 'friends with benefits.' It went on fine for nearly a year, and everyone thought that they were a couple.

 It was nearly after a year that her behavior towards him started to change. She declared that she had fallen in love with him and wanted commitment. It was around the same time that he met Sakshi and fell in love with her. It was a very difficult situation for him. He wanted to break up with Anu and get committed to Sakshi, whereas Anu was pressuring him for commitment.

He tried to be gentle with Anu. He told her that he had never promised her commitment. They were both in the relationship because they both wanted it. She still persisted. He finally had to tell her that he was in love with Sakshi. Anu took it in a really bad way, and the next few months were hell for him and Sakshi.

Thinking about that phase still gave him shivers.

But all the bad blood between them could not erase the happy memories that they had shared. He did not want to pick up another fight with her, but he had no option. He was fully aware that his phone call would again ruffle her up. He remembered the way she had reacted when he had called the last time.

She picked up on the second ring as if she was waiting for his call.

"I was wondering when you would call," she said, as she switched off the video mode.

"Can I not see your face, Anu?" He tried to start gently.

"No, tell me what you have to say and get lost," she said. "Though I already know what you will say."

"Look Anu, before I talk to your friend, I wanted to talk to you. Perhaps you can knock some sense in him. I have no objection to his absurd idea. The only thing I ask is that he should not make it political. That will be detrimental for him." He spoke very calmly and placed special emphasis on the word 'detrimental.'

"Are you threatening me?" She asked.

"Anu, you know that I don't threaten. I act. Just try to make him understand. I have come to know that Ekta Party has approached him. They will use him as a pawn in this game of chess. I know you are wise enough to understand this, and I hope you care enough for him to make him understand," he kept his voice as gentle as possible.

"Just fuck off! I don't care what you think. I will do no such thing as 'counselling' him. Rather, if it adversely affects your party, I will encourage him. Don't you dare call me again," she replied in a harsh voice. He could hear the venom in her words.

"Then I will deal with him in my own way, which might not be good for either of you, okay? Don't complain that I did not warn you." He disconnected the call and kept staring at his phone, thinking about how he should deal with the problem with minimum collateral damage.

Anu had been in her room, getting ready for bed, when she had received Sooraj's call.

She was fuming when she disconnected the call. This man was too much! 'How dare he call me again,' she thought.

After Sooraj had betrayed her for Sakshi, she had gone into severe depression. She did not even feel like thinking about it. After seeing a psychiatrist for months, she had somewhat recovered and slowly limped back to life. She still had to take the pills though. If she forgot to take her pills, she would get a severe headache and would go into depression. This was all Sooraj's fault. He had broken her heart.

Years had passed, and she had now made a new life for herself. Her NGO was her passion, and she wanted to spread the message of love and peace in the world. She had her life chalked out, and things were happening as per plan. She was not satisfied with the NGO only, though. Her dreams were big. Really big! So big that sometimes they scared her. Sometimes, her own thoughts scared her. But she knew, nothing and no one would stop her from achieving what she wished for.

Peace between the warring countries would be a major achievement not only for her NGO but also for the common people. Precious lives would not be wasted anymore. Karan's father had unknowingly set a wheel in motion, and it was now gaining momentum. This was a wheel of change. She was very excited.

However, when she thought about why Karan was doing all this, she did not feel good. She tried to block that aspect from her mind. Perhaps for Karan too, it was not about his love anymore. She also noticed that he did not talk about Fiza as often as he earlier used to.

How did he think he would adjust with a Pakistani anyway? All said and done, they are culturally so different from us, she thought.

Anu opened her drawer and took out her palmtop. She opened a folder that she had recently created. All the images were on the screen. The pictures they had taken together. The pictures of him that she had saved as screenshots while talking on the phone, the pictures she had clicked without his knowledge. All the images were there, Karan in different moods. Some smiling, some frowning, some with that intense look when he was trying to make a point, some with the soft look and starry eyes, perhaps when he was talking to or about Fiza, thought Anu with a grimace.

Anu initially started this habit of clicking his pictures as she thought he was very photogenic, but lately, she found that she liked looking at his pictures. In fact, she liked being with him, talking to him, thinking about him and talking about him.

In Chhabua village, she had casually mentioned about sharing a room, which he had laughed off. At that time, it was just about sex. Things seemed different today.

'Am I falling in love with him or am I already in love with him?' She wondered.

She did not like this thought. Look what love got her last time. She had lost precious time of her life grieving for a relationship that was not meant to be, and hankering for a person who did not care about her.

'I should not be thinking like this,' she chided herself. 'I cannot fall for any man right now, least of all for a man who is already taken.'

'I have a bigger purpose in my life. Being someone's girlfriend or wife is certainly not in the big picture. I cannot get diverted from my main motive. I cannot lose focus,' she thought.

"I simply cannot afford another breakdown. I have to get him out of my mind," she actually spoke aloud.

"Anu, love was not made for you. Forget Karan and focus on your purpose." It was as if she was trying to pacify the innocent heart that refused to listen to reason and logic.

Anu added that day's image from her phone to the folder in her palmtop and kept it inside the drawer again. She was feeling slightly more in control now.

He can remain a friend or a flame, but not a lover. He was really in love with Fiza.

'But people fall out of love, don't they?' She asked herself. Sooraj had perhaps never loved her, but she had loved him from the bottom of her heart. Did she not fall out of love with him? She did. So everything is possible. Moreover, for how long will they be able to maintain a long distance relationship? It was getting difficult. She saw that many times he was unable to even take her calls. Fiza was always so finicky about her name being dragged into any controversy. The pace at which Karan was gaining popularity, the day was not far when journalists would dig into his past and discover Fiza. How would she feel then?

If Fiza herself went out of his life, it would be very easy to get into Karan's life. A heartbroken person is very vulnerable and susceptible. They both got along very well together. He liked her too. She was sure of it.

'Oh, why am I thinking about all this? I should instead focus on the problem in hand,' she again reminded herself.

Sooraj getting threatened by Karan and their movement was something very significant. He was not a man who got into the defensive mode easily. Though he was not entirely aggressive, he did actually give them a veiled threat! Karan was catching people's attention for sure. He had shared with her that someone named Sandy from Ekta Party had called, wanting to meet him. He had then taken her along for the meeting. They had met Sandy over coffee, and Karan had ruled out any kind of alliance with any political party.

"I am not here to get into politics. I could have done this when I was in college. I am here to bring peace between the two countries." He had very firmly closed all the discussions.

While leaving, Sandy gave her his visiting card asking her to call him if Karan changed his mind.

"I am not Karan's secretary," she had said. She felt like giving it back to him, but then changed her mind and slipped the card inside her bag.

How would she ensure that they could continue with their movement, and at the same time, also make sure that Karan remained safe? She knew what Sooraj was capable of. He could go to any extent to safeguard his own interests. If they made a pact with Ekta Party, Karan's life would be in danger! Sooraj was very ambitious, and he would not let anything come between him and his ambitions.

The moment she thought of Karan's life being in danger, she had a sinking feeling in her heart.

It was at that moment that she realized without any iota of doubt, that the damage was already done. She was in love with Karan!

That was the moment when the *bindaas* girl with a devil-may-care attitude suddenly felt very vulnerable and defenseless. She felt an amazing feeling of tenderness towards Karan whenever she thought of him. True, he did not love her, but that did not stop her from loving him.

She felt her eyes go moist and a single tear trickled down from her eye. She buried her face in the pillow and let the tears flow.

Love hurts! It hurts real bad! Who would know this better than her? After everything that she had faced the last time, why did she have to fall in love again?

'Will I let love destroy all that I have built over the years again? God, I don't want to love him. Either make him fall in love with me or make me fall out of love! Why are you so cruel, God?'

That night, yet another woman cried in her pillow, pining for her unrequited love, praying to and pleading with God to make him hers.

The next morning, Anu woke up with a headache and a sinking heart. All that crying last night had given her swollen eyes and a splitting headache.

She searched her drawer for a painkiller. She was about to pop it in, but then she remembered that she had skipped dinner last night. It was not a good idea to take a painkiller on an empty stomach.

She got up from the bed, and while looking for her slippers, she advanced towards the kitchen. The kitchen was a mess as she hardly ever cooked. She mostly ate out or skipped meals. The coffee maker was the only machine that she used daily. She switched it on and waited for her coffee.

She rummaged in her refrigerator and took out a packet of 'heat and serve parathas'. A look at the expiry date told her what she already knew. She threw it in the dustbin. There was no bread but she found some eggs. She took two out and put them in the egg boiler. That was the quickest breakfast possible.

By the time the eggs were ready, she took out a couple of cookies from the cookie box. Putting the cookies, the boiled eggs and the coffee on a tray, she went back to her bed.

The headache was getting worse. So, she quickly ate her breakfast and gulped down the coffee. Then, she took her medicine and slipped inside the bed covers again.

She lay there quietly for some time when there was a call on her phone. It was Karan's friend, Vivek, on the line. For a moment, she thought of not taking the call, but by now, she was feeling much better, and she also wanted to speak to Vivek about the new development. So, she took the call in audio mode.

 "Hi, Vivek. What's happening? Where is your friend?" She asked, trying to sound casual.

"A lot is happening and you also know about it, Anu. I wanted to talk to you about it. I came to know about your meeting with a party worker from Ekta Party."

"True, and he was offered a position in the party which he refused," she completed what he was about to say.

"I don't think we should have rejected the offer," Vivek continued. "They are very powerful people, and they have a very good chance of coming to power after the upcoming elections. He need not have joined them, but certain alliances with them would have definitely helped our cause."

"Did you tell this to your friend?" She asked calmly, already knowing the answer.

"Yes, but he will not listen to me," he said. "That's why I want your help. Please tell him not to offend powerful people."

"Oh, and here I was thinking of talking to you for the same help. What makes you think that he will listen to me?" Anu was curious.

"He listens to you more than he listens to me these days. Though, I agree that he can be very stubborn once he makes up his mind. But I thought there was no harm in trying."

Vivek's words felt like a soothing balm on her heart that was hurting. Did Karan really listen to her, she wondered.

"Vivek, I too wanted to talk to you about him. In fact, there was a new development last night which has me worried,"

Anu suddenly sounded serious as she thought of the reason why she wanted to talk to him in the first place.

"What is it? Don't tell me that he has made a pass at you when I have been wanting to do that for a long time," Vivek joked.

"Vivek, I received a call from my ex-boyfriend who is now with Hindu Maha Morcha," Anu ignored the flirtatious interest that Vivek was showing. He somehow got to know that an Ekta Party worker had a meeting with us. God knows from where they got the information. He kind of threatened us that Karan should not get associated with Ekta Party, otherwise there would be consequences. I know him. He is dangerous, and so, it has got me worried," Anu finally blurted out what had been bothering her since the previous night.

"What the fuck! They threatened us? Actually threatened us? This means we are getting under their skin," he somehow sounded more excited and less worried!

"Aren't you worried?" Anu was aghast!

"Look, Karan was always the one to play with danger. Even in college, he ruffled many feathers, and when he refused to join any political party, he annoyed some political goons as well. All this never bothered him. I know him; he is a person who can swim against the current if he believes in something," Vivek tried to justify his lack of concern when he heard the bewilderment in Anu's voice. "Nevertheless, I personally believe that he should join Ekta Party, because what he is out to achieve is not possible without political backing." He came back to the purpose for which he had called.

"I agree, and to be honest, I am a little disturbed by this threat. I know that man, and he is capable of anything!" A dark shadow passed over her face as she was reminded of her unpleasant past.

"It's a tricky situation. Ekta Party will be offended if he doesn't join them, and Hindu Maha Morcha will be a danger if he does join them," Vivek pondered over the situation.

"True," Anu agreed and disconnected the call.

'What has he started? Where has he landed himself?' Anu could not get rid of the uneasy feeling that was gnawing at her heart.

'What will you do, my friend? What will you do?' Anu mentally asked Karan, who was nowhere near her to answer the question.

PAKISTAN HIGH COMMISSION CHANAKYAPURI, NEW DELHI 2/50-G, SHANTIPATH,

The room was well lit with two beautiful chandeliers hanging from the roof. Even though the lighting had changed with the modern, pea-sized LED bulbs replacing the old ones, the chandeliers still found their place, and because of their age-old charm and the royal look, they added to the ambience. There were three sets of antique sofas in the different corners of the room. After the chandeliers, the most eye-catching item was the huge teak wood table that was placed in the center of the room. The dark brown color with the gold polish in the corners added to its majestic look.

Ahmed Razak was sitting on the massive chair that was placed alongside the table. He had a small frame, and with his head bent down in files, he somehow managed to get camouflaged in his surroundings. But that was only as long as his head was bent down because the moment he looked up, one could not fail to notice his intelligent features. The sharp nose and grey eyes that stared from behind the gold-rimmed spectacles were features one could not easily forget. What he lacked in his frame was more than made up by the authoritative and intense look on his face.

Ahmed was a force to reckon with. He had to be, as he was an ambassador to an enemy state. This was not a mean task. In a career spanning more than 20 years and across many countries, this was the most challenging assignment he had been given. He was made the Pakistani ambassador to India when the times were very volatile. There was tension across the border. Of course, the situation was mostly like this but lately, with elections around the corner in India, the situation had deteriorated.

Ahmed had to ensure that Pakistan's interest in India was taken care of. He had his own sources, and he kept a tab on the pulse of the nation. Things, though turbulent, were still under his control.

He worked hard to ensure this. He wanted to do his job sincerely, and at the same time, did not want to be collateral damage in the political brawl between the two nations. He was always extra cautious in safeguarding both the interests of his nation and his career.

He finished his work and was about to buzz his secretary to dictate some final notes and call it a day. His wife was hosting a party today, and all the Pakistani diplomats in Delhi were invited. A famous ghazal singer from Pakistan, Zareen Khan, would be performing at the party. Just then, his phone rang. This was the 'safe' line on which he did not get calls very often. It was directly from the Pakistani Prime Minister's office. He looked at the door to ensure that it was closed, and then he took the call.

"As-Salaam-Alaikum", he said and listened carefully to what the other person had to say.

"*Hann, janaab,*" he replied respectfully. "From what my sources tell me, he has come from London, and he has this weird idea of uniting India and Pakistan on the 100th year of partition. He seems to be a lunatic, but he has garnered a huge following and is holding mass rallies."

Ahmed paused as the person on the other side started talking. He flinched a couple of times, which meant that the conversation was not very pleasant.

"*Janaab*, I will take care and I will not take him lightly. You will have a complete report on him by tomorrow evening."

He kept repeating "*Ji janaab*" in affirmation as the person on the other side continued giving instructions.

After a while, he kept the phone down with a hint of sweat shining on his forehead.

'I guess I failed to gauge the seriousness of the situation,' he thought. Of course, he had kept this man, Karan, under supervision, but he had never thought he would start to ruffle feathers in Pakistan too. A phone from the High Command was serious business.

It was true that if a lunatic like Karan could reach out and touch the raw nerve of the common people, it was possible that the public would also start talking peace and unity. This was certainly not in favor of any political party. Governments on both sides had traditionally thrived on the enmity between the two countries. Likewise, political parties on either side of the border stood to lose if the public started talking about peace and unity. Wiping his brow with a napkin, Ahmed forgot all about the party at home and got to work, making calls to various numbers from the 'safe' line. Numbers that he called were not stored anywhere except in his memory!

After the call from Fiza in which she had clearly hinted at breaking up with him, Karan had become very particular about calling her up daily. He tried to avoid talking about the current situation that he was in, but he was so immersed in all the happenings that he sometimes felt at a loss for topics to talk about with her. This had never happened before, but it was happening now, only because he was trying not to tell her about the recent developments that were taking place at a very fast pace. She would unnecessarily worry if she came to know that there was a threat to his life from the Hindu Maha Morcha.

Sometimes, he would feel lost and wonder if the path that he was walking on would ever actually take him to his destination. Why didn't he simply marry Fiza and bring her to meet his family later? But he knew the answer to this. He would never do anything to hurt his father. Moreover, he was a person who always took the uncharted road.

Karan could not sleep and kept tossing and turning on the bed. Finally, he got up and went to the terrace. Dawn was breaking, yet the morning sun had not arrived. The birds were singing their morning chorus. This is what he loved about old Delhi. It had retained its old charm and did not get lost in the rampant development like the other parts of the city. It was maintained like a heritage place with lots of greenery around.

He sat on his favorite rocking chair and closed his eyes. He reflected on the events that had happened so rapidly and also started to plan in his mind for the future course of action.

He had almost dozed off when his ringing phone brought him out of his reverie. It was a call from their Lajpat Nagar's office number. He looked at the watch. It was five in the morning.

'Who could be calling from the office this early in the morning?' He wondered.

"Sir, please come soon." He guessed it was the guard. "Our office has been robbed." The panic in his voice was clear.

Karan jumped off the chair he was dozing in just a few seconds ago. Who would rob their office?

There was hardly anything of value. Perhaps some local thieves were trying their luck, he surmised.

He took his car keys and left. Everyone was sleeping, and so, he just stepped out quietly, closing the door softly behind him.

Karan called up Vivek and Anu on the way and informed them about the incident. They too said that they would reach there straightaway.

When Karan arrived at the location, he found the office door open. He called out the guard's name and entered the room. Suddenly, someone pounced on him, and he was thrown on the ground. Before he could say anything, he was hit by something on his head. A shearing intense pain shot through him, and he passed out. He must have come back to his senses immediately for he saw two masked men, in the room, ready to hit him again. This time they used their legs to kick him in his stomach. He cried out for help, but it came out more like a whimper than a scream. Blood was oozing from his head. The blow was so hard that it might have cracked a bone. He was in great pain, unable to scream or move, but his mind was working. Vivek and Anu would be here soon. He should try to remain alive.

As if they read his mind, one of them said, "We can kill you if we want, but we don't want to make you a hero or a martyr. This is just a warning. Go back to where you have come from and forget all about what you are doing here. If you don't listen to us, next time we will not hesitate in making you a martyr." They both laughed and launched one more kick at his stomach as they went out of the door. Karan looked at his phone, which was broken into pieces. He made an unsuccessful attempt to crawl out and call for help, but it was too much of an effort and he passed out.

He opened his eyes to find himself on a hospital bed. His head was in a plaster, and the excruciating pain had somehow subsided. He opened his eyes and saw Anu sitting on a chair on his right. He looked at her, and from her eyes, he could tell that she had been crying. He tried moving his head to turn towards her, but an agonizing pain stopped him. Anu, by now, had noticed that he was awake. She stood up at once to talk to him. She held his hand in her hands and said, "Thank God you are fine." A little tear rolled down her cheeks, and she made no effort to wipe it away.

"How are you feeling?" She asked.

Karan just gestured with his hand that he was fine.

"The call was a ploy to get you there. They had handcuffed the guard and locked him up in a room and then used the office phone to call you," she filled him in. "You are lucky to be alive!" This time the tears fell like rain.

"Why are you crying? I am fine. They have only succeeded in making me more determined to continue my work," Karan managed to speak slowly. "Whoever they were, they did not know that intimidation is not the way to get at me. It makes my resolve stronger."

"We will have to be careful, only the other day I got a threat, and now this!" She was in better control now.

"Anu, I have to ask you a favor," Karan whispered.

"Anything…" she said, as she bent down to listen to what he wanted to say.

"I think I will be out of action for a week or so. Till that time, I request you to take charge of the entire movement and spearhead the campaign. Nothing should slow us down now." He looked at her with resolve in his eyes, but his hands were gentle as he reached out and touched hers.

"If that is what you want, then we won't slow down, I promise," she replied as she gave his hand a gentle squeeze of reassurance.

Next day, Anu called an emergency meeting of the core group. Karan was still hospitalized, but he was recovering speedily.

They all assembled in their office in the evening. Vivek had a ferocious look on his face and was avoiding eye contact with Anu. Just a few days back, he had been excited at the mention of the threat to Karan's life. He had taken it so very lightly. He would never have thought that it would come true.

Anu started the meeting by expressing her anguish at the physical assault on Karan and also spoke about the security concerns. It was decided that the security aspects would need a revamp.

Then she came to the main point. She told the members that Karan's resolve had strengthened after this incident, and he had asked her to take the lead in his absence.

 "I have thought a lot about it. This is the right time to start a very aggressive campaign. Even though, as per our plan, it was to come later, I suggest that we should jump into the fire now! This unexpected and unfortunate incident can be used to our advantage. We will go to the masses and tell them that this is the reward one gets for talking about peace in this country! What do you all think?" She sought their opinion.

They all were quiet for a few moments as if trying to weigh the pros and cons. Vivek was the first one to speak up. He spoke slowly as if he was evaluating every word before uttering it.

"Just a few days back, Anu received a threat. The person had told her to warn Karan against doing what he was doing. Anu was disturbed, but I took it very lightly. Now, of course, we know that it was not an empty threat. Knowing my friend, I knew such a thing will only further strengthen his resolve, and this is exactly what has happened. He will not stop, but we cannot let him be in any danger. Keeping all this in mind, we need to plan our new strategy. I think we should become very aggressive with our campaigning and tell the people what has happened. After the news of the attack is made public, we will garner public sympathy, and they will think twice before getting violent again."

Everyone listened to what he had to say without interrupting. Then, it was Sumit who interrupted. "What if they do something and make it look like an accident?" He had said something that had been on everyone's mind.

"That is unlikely but possible. We will have to be very careful and not leave Karan alone. One of us should always be with him." He said.

Everyone nodded in agreement.

Anu glanced at Sumit who looked lost in his thoughts. "I think you have already started working on our promotion strategy," she smiled. He never failed to impress her with his immense knowledge and commitment towards digital marketing.

"I will be ready with a plan by tomorrow evening and will make a presentation so that you can approve," he smiled in response.

The next evening, when they met, a detailed plan was chalked out, which included digital media promotions, talk shows, road shows, addressing the college students, candle-light procession for peace etc.

Everyone was very impressed by Sumit's detailed analysis. He had also shortlisted the names of the partners with whom they would associate.

They decided to first start with social media promotion along with a meeting at India Gate to protest against this violence and to talk about peace. They decided to hold the meeting the following week itself when Karan would be in a position to attend it and at the same time, look like a victim of a violent attack.

This meeting had to be highly publicized so that the turnout would be good. Various media contacts would be roped in, and they would get good coverage.

It was Anu who proposed that instead of having speeches in the meeting, they should have a musical concert where they would have a few short speeches along with songs on love and peace.

Everyone loved this idea, and they discussed and debated on it further. They kept working till late evening, planning, discussing and minutely going over each detail. Roles were assigned. Teams were formed, and they all worked from their hearts to fulfill their friend's mission, which had now become their own!

No one had ever thought that the turnout in the mass rally would be so huge. The campaign was very successful. They all had toiled hard, day and night, to make it a success.

The roadshow group was doing more than ten shows every day in various parts of the city. No college was left unattended. They were able to garner support from all quarters.

Karan's aunt, Sunidhi, was heading the group of ladies, and she was holding meetings with various women's clubs. Posters were being made which had Karan's picture on the hospital bed, with various slogans.

 "Don't talk about peace, or else you will become a target of violence."

"Don't talk about love, or else you will become a victim of hate."

In the conferences and discussions, they talked about how the love for a Pakistani girl had been the genesis of this movement. "Love is very powerful; it has the power to make history," They argued their case. "We have had enough wars; let's give love a chance. We parted with hatred; let's unite with love." These slogans were frequently used in their talks.

The media was soaking everything up, and the love story behind the entire campaign only added to its romanticism. Many people were inquisitive about the identity of the girl, but no one knew anything about her. So, the media called her the "mystery woman".

Sunita and Ajay had also come from Chhabua. They had anyway wanted to leave behind the city that reminded them of the gruesome mass murders. They moved to Delhi, and Ajay took up a job in Vivek's printing press. They also attended various meetings, and Sunita became a very good speaker. The pain of grief she carried in her eyes could only be communicated by a person who had gone through a living hell. Often, her speeches would leave a majority of the listeners misty-eyed.

All these efforts resulted in a huge gathering at the India Gate.

The evening started with them singing a song from an old Amitabh Bachhan movie. This was Vivek's favorite song.

'*Kitne baju kitnesar, gin le dushman dhyan se*

Jeetenge hum har baazi, jab khele hum jeejaan se"

Karan was on the stage along with Anu and a few singers that they had arranged for the event. Two of them were famous Bollywood singers, and their presence pulled a bigger crowd. They sang one song after the other. All songs were about love and peace.

This was a first-of-its-kind public meeting for a cause which was done in the form of a musical concert. Between the songs, Anu spoke about their mission. She spoke about the threat they had received without naming anybody. She spoke about how Karan was beaten up by forces who did not want them to talk about peace or unity.

Then, Karan came on stage. He was not in a position to speak much, because his vocal cord had suffered injuries during the attack, but he managed to at least, be there physically on the stage, which had a huge effect. The doctor had said it would take at least a couple of more weeks for proper speech to be restored. He simply waved at the public and thanked them for their support. The crowd went mad, and they started chanting his name.

Karan. Karan. Karan…they went on in chorus. Karan felt that he was living a dream. It seemed so surreal. He could not believe that in just a few months, they had gathered so much public support. This only proved one point. The common people were sick of wars, and they wanted peace now. 'The boundaries will go one day. Maybe not immediately, but the seeds have been sown,' he mused. 'Time will come a full circle when, after 100 years of partition, which were full of violence, hatred and destruction, there will be union which will be fueled by love, peace, and understanding.'

A voice in his mind said, "Do it." It was on the spur of the moment that he made an important announcement.

In his faltering voice, he said, "A few months from now, on 15th August 2047, we will be completing our 100 years of independence and also partition. We propose to have a peace walk from Delhi to Islamabad. Details will be shared with you. The common public in both the countries wants peace. It is high time that we raise our voices and be heard!"

There was a moment of pin drop silence as if people were trying to absorb what was just said. Then, all hell broke loose as everyone started yelling and shouting in support.

Nothing could be heard except the chanting of his name…Karan. Karan. Karan. More than the public, the team members were in shock. They had not decided on anything like this. What had come over Karan? How could he even think of doing such a thing? It would need a lot of political support to get the permissions for such an event. They were all wondering what had gotten into his mind for him to have made such an announcement without even discussing it with them! They did not say anything though they joined in the mass chanting of the name of their leader.

The event that was supposed to end at eleven went on till past midnight.

After the event, they were all so drained that they decided to stop all activities for the next two days and take complete rest. However, after Karan's announcement, they were hounded by the media, which wanted to know in detail about their plan. They wanted a press briefing, but that was not possible because they themselves had not discussed the plan! Karan had immediately left after the event, and no one had had a chance to speak with him.

The next morning, Karan was still in bed when Fiza called. Karan had been discharged from the hospital only a couple of days back, and he still felt weak. The exertions from the previous night had also been exhausting, and so, he had decided to sleep off the whole day. He took her call, eyes still closed. She had been very upset to know that he had been attacked. Karan did not want her to know this, but once they had decided that they would use this attack to their advantage for getting sympathy, there was no way he could have hidden this news from her. It was all over social media. The musical mass rally was the trending news.

He was a little nervous talking to her, but there was no other alternative. "How are you?" She asked. She was wearing a light green T-shirt and a pair of black pajamas. She was sitting on her rocking chair and was sipping something, perhaps some energy drink.

"I am following the news in the media. When were you planning to tell me about the peace walk from Delhi to Islamabad? After it was over?" Fiza did not beat around the bush but came straight to the point.

"Sweetheart, it was only yesterday that I decided this. It was a spur of the moment decision for me," he told her the truth, but she would have none of it.

"Karan, it is not possible! I am anything but a fool! You kept me in the dark. Now it is not about us anymore. You have become crazy about this dream of yours. I will have none of it," she was furious. "You are already making enemies. I have a strong feeling that you will join some political party very soon. I did not want this. You know that I hate politics. I always have!" She was unstoppable.

"Listen, believe me when I say this, I have not even discussed this with my team. In fact, they must be furious with me too. We haven't even got the time to talk about it yet. I am as scared to face them as I was to talk to you, but this happens to be true," he said. "If you don't believe me, I am adding

Anu in this call, you can ask her," he continued, and before she could protest, he called Anu. She picked up at the first ring as if she had been waiting for his call, and without noticing that it was a conference call and Fiza was also on the line, she shouted at Karan.

"Karan, have you gone mad? How could you make such an announcement without even telling us?"

"See, I told you the truth. No one knew until that moment," he said, "Not even me," he said softly, as if feeling guilty about it.

It was then that Anu realized that Fiza was also on the line. "Hi Fiza," she said.

"Hi," Fiza replied absentmindedly. Her thoughts were still on the ramifications of the way the things were unfolding.

"Look Karan, you know very well that my aunt is in politics. I cannot afford my name being dragged into this. She has done a lot for me, and I can't put her into any situation which is bad for her career. She sent me away from Pakistan, because I could not live the way she wanted me to live. Her career means a lot to her, and I can't jeopardize that. If back home it is known that Fatima Akhtar's niece is the reason behind all this drama about peace and union, hell will break loose! I have a strong feeling that very soon some journalist will dig out my name and identity, and I dread to think what will happen next. So, please stop all this and come back to me," she said, trying to push back her tears, and in the process, sniffing quietly.

Anu quietly kept the phone down lost in her own thoughts.

Neither Karan nor Fiza noticed that Anu had left the conversation.

Fiza was openly sobbing now, and Karan was trying to console her. He felt a surge of tender emotions and wanted to take her in his arms and kiss the tears away. He felt so helpless. The person for whom he had started this movement was hurt and desperately wanted him to stop.

He knew that this option was no more an option now. He had come a long way, and there was no turning back. Not that he wanted to. Fiza was right when she said that it was no longer about them. It wasn't. It had become much more than a promise made to his father to win the girl he loved. It was about what he was searching for all his life — his calling. It was about making a mark in history. It was about writing history.

He tried to convince Fiza that he had taken all precautions and that her identity would remain a secret.

"Even if they manage to find out about you, they will not be able to trace it to your aunt because you yourself have kept your family name a secret. No one in London is aware of your connection to your aunt. So, how will they ever be able to connect you to her? Don't be hyper," he was gentle yet firm with her.

With so many things happening at the same time, he could not handle a hysterical girlfriend. After talking to her for nearly an hour and convincing her that it would soon be over and that her name would not be dragged into the mess, he finally managed to soothe her raw nerves, but in the process gave himself a splitting headache!

ISLAMABAD

When Riyaz had started working for the movement in Islamabad, he had thought that his work would be very difficult, and it would be very difficult for him to get support. He had also feared political backlash if the news reached influential people. So, he had tried to start it in a very a tentative manner. His trepidation turned out to be false. Unlike what he had thought, the reaction from the youth was very positive. After all, it was their future that was at stake every time there was a war, and they had to sacrifice their lives.

Riyaz did not speak about uniting India and Pakistan upfront, but he talked about bringing peace between the two countries and then, if things improved, union of the two countries could also be explored.

Riyaz kept in touch with Karan and Anu in India, and with Fiza in London. Fiza would take regular updates and never failed to remind him that her name should not be linked with Karan in the current situation.

Riyaz was careful enough to keep things low-key. Unlike in India, where Karan had become a hero, people did not know about Riyaz in Islamabad. He preferred to work on a one-to-one basis. He had already formed an organization, '*Awaam ki awaaz*,' the voice of the nation.

'I am operating more like a terrorist organization,' he chuckled to himself. Ironically, talking of peace between the two countries was always risky, and at times, he felt vulnerable.

But very soon, he would have to be bold and come out in the open. The support that he was getting from the youth was giving him confidence.

He was planning to have his first public meeting very soon. With Karan announcing his peace walk, there was no alternative but to come out in the open.

He had contacted the media channels, which were not so liberal in their views but agreed to talk with him. He was ready with his speech and also with the action plan to take things forward openly.

What he dreaded the most was to tell his mother about all this. She would panic when she would get to know about his involvement in this movement. She had already declared that Karan was a mad man, playing with fire. She would never agree to his jumping into this fire as well.

Riyaz was sitting on the floor watching TV when the news about Karan flashed on the TV. The Pakistani media were calling him a crazy person, and they also alleged that he was affiliated to the Ekta Party, which was using him for their political gains. Ekta Party just wanted to get the Muslim votes in India, the news claimed.

His mom was also sitting beside him, peeling potatoes. "If he is your friend, knock some sense into him. Why does he want to die young?" She said, without taking her eyes off the TV.

"Why do you say this, *ammi*? Don't you want peace between the two countries? Won't it be nice if we become one again? You will be able to visit the town where you grew up as a child. No one will treat you as an outsider ever," he tried to test the waters before disclosing the truth to her.

"It's a pipe dream Riyaz. There can never be peace between the two countries because the people in power will never allow it. It suits them to keep the fire of hatred burning. They fuel it so that no one even thinks of peace. Even today, they talk of things that happened years ago. They want to keep this issue alive," she had a sad look on her face and keeping the bowl of potatoes aside, turned towards Riyaz as if involuntarily preparing herself for what was coming next.

"*Ammi*, what Karan is doing there, I am trying to do here, albeit on a smaller scale," he said, looking straight into her eyes.

She was quiet. Her eyes welled up with tears.

"I knew it in my heart. This is why you left everything and came here. Why Riyaz, why? You know I have no one else in this world except you," she was sobbing openly now.

"*Ammi,* if we want a better world, someone will have to at least start talking about it. I know, it is risky, but someone will have to take that risk. Someone will have to make sacrifices. I am a part of *jehaad, ammi.* This is a war for peace. You need to help me, *ammi.* Make me strong and not weak." Riyaz took her sobbing *ammi* in his arms and rocked her like a child.

NEW DELHI

This was one of the quiet cafés of Saket. The prices were exorbitant, and so, it was hardly ever crowded. For people who went there, the ambience made it worthwhile. Every seating was different and special. There were some sofas, some rocking chairs, some cane *modhas*, some cane chairs and many small *jhoolas* where you could sit and sip your drink.

Anu was sitting on the rocking chair, facing the garden outside. She had ordered her favorite iced tea and was sipping it slowly as if savoring every sip. Whenever her mind was in chaos and she felt like indulging herself, she came here, which was not very often.

She always came here alone. This 'me' time at this place was sacrosanct to her. She did not feel like sharing it with anyone.

Today, she had come here after a very long time. There were many things going on in her mind, some of which she did not want to dwell upon even with her own self. The fact that Karan had made such a major announcement without consulting her had made her furious. She felt like grabbing him by his neck and giving him a shake. Good that they did not meet immediately after the event. Time had pacified her, and she had started to think with a straight mind.

Perhaps it was for good that it was announced without much deliberation. Sometimes when a lot of deliberations go into a discussion, the decision becomes weak. Certain decisions have to be taken at the spur of the moment and then the way forward can be planned. The more she thought about it, the more convinced she became that it was the best thing to happen under the circumstances.

Now that the decision was made, they needed to take it forward. This would require enormous planning and organizing. She had spoken to Riyaz in Islamabad a few days back. Things had started to move at a faster pace there as well.

The time was ripe. With elections around the corner, this was the time to make a mark. But for them to execute such an ambitious project, they needed political support. The offer from Ekta Party should have been taken. Even now it was open for them. Just the day before, Sandy had contacted her again and had requested them to join hands with his party.

They wanted to make use of the huge fan following that Karan was enjoying. The public sentiment was with him, especially after the attack. After the musical event, they had been receiving emails and messages in hordes. Everyone wanted to be a part of the historic march to Islamabad.

The alliance would do them good too. They would get better financial support, and administrative arrangements would also be taken care of. Yes, this was not something they could pull off on their own. Also, if the mass rally was successful, there would be danger sirens both in Delhi and in Islamabad. She was sure if the Ekta Party came to power, they would offer Karan some very important portfolio. She herself was offered an assured portfolio if such an alliance took place. Not that she was interested in anything of that sort. She was happy running her NGO, and she had bigger plans. Karan, on the other hand, needed the support if he truly wanted to make a mark in history. Unfortunately, he was against any political alliance. She would have to try and convince Karan again. Yes, she would talk to him again, and soon!

Anu finished her tea and swiped her phone to make the payment. She picked up her *jhola* and with determination in her eyes, walked out of the café.

She jumped on her bike and zoomed off! She suddenly knew what she had to do. She dictated a message to Karan from her wristwatch phone.

"Meet me at The Garden restaurant at the earliest. I have something urgent to discuss," she sent the message and rerouted her bike towards the restaurant.

It was just a few months back that she had come here to meet Karan. A lot had happened in those months. A lot more was to happen. She went to a pink cabana and ordered another iced tea as she waited for Karan. She knew he would come. He was much better now, and he was at home.

About thirty minutes later, she saw that familiar face. Her heart missed a beat. Why did this happen every time she met him? For a moment, she forgot all that she had to say to him, and instead started thinking about how handsome he looked. He was wearing a black t-shirt and blue denims. The smile on his face, when he looked at her, just took her breath away. She chided herself mentally, 'Stay calm and focused Anu, you have a lot in your hands.'

"Hi Anu. What happened, dear? Why this rush?" As expected, Karan was full of questions.

"Relax. I wanted some peace and quiet with you, so I called you here. This is where we had our first date," she said.

"Date? You know it was not a date, Anu," he said and immediately noticed that her face fell. "It was a historic moment when the two of us planned to change the course of history," he quickly said, bringing the smile back on her face.

"Look Karan, we need to rethink about the offer we received from Ekta Party. Currently, an alliance with them is what we need to meet our objectives," Anu wanted to continue speaking, but Karan cut her short and did not let her finish. "No, that is out of the question," he said firmly.

"Karan, listen to me first before you make the final decision. I supported your decision of not joining hands with them at that point of time. Things have changed. Suddenly, everything has moved to a faster gear. You have promised to walk to Islamabad in August. There are hardly a few months left. How do you think that will be possible? We need political support. We need funds. We need them, Karan. It's not the opposite. It is very likely that they will come to power this time. Be practical Karan, not ideological."

Karan was very quiet. For a moment, Anu thought that she had made her mark, but then the subsequent look on his face told a different story.

"No Anu. A hundred times, no. I have promised myself never to make this political. I have promised Fiza the same. It was never about power. It was about peace. Whatever you say, even you know that if we join them, we will not be 'us' anymore. They are a bigger organization. They are a political organization. They will swallow us. They will ride to victory on our name and our mission; our ambition will vanish into thin air.

"We at least don't have enemies today. There are people who feel threatened by us, but since we are not a political party yet, they are still somewhat comforted. The day we join a political party, the opposition parties become our enemies. Dirt will be dug out from our past. Our families will be made the victims. Most importantly, sooner or later, Fiza's name will get dragged into this."

Anu kept listening to him. He was in no mood to stop.

"I have started this dream, this mission and will take it to a logical conclusion. People have started talking about peace. People have started thinking about the union. Seeds of change have been sown. I will do my duty. Once this walk concludes, I will withdraw from the public eye. I will marry Fiza and go back to London. I am sure after seeing all my efforts, my father will give his blessings to our marriage," he said.

"No, Anu, I will not join any political party, and this is my final decision." Karan seemed agitated as he got up and walked away. Anu kept staring at his receding back.

She did not stop him. He needed time to cool down, and she needed time to think.

NEWHAM, LONDON

When and how the Almighty up there decides to bring a twist in the tales, we mortals have no clue. It is only much later, when we reflect back on the events, that we realize how a single incident changed the course of our lives.

The day started just like any other day. When Fiza got up in the morning, she had no inkling that this day would change her life forever. Like every day, she had woken up late. She rushed through the morning chores and was just about to grab the coffee that Felicia had made for her, when her phone rang. She thought it was Karan and decided to talk to him later from her car. But then, she saw that the call was not from India but Islamabad, and it was none other than her *khala* calling!

She had a sense of foreboding and knew that it was not going to be good news. *khala* never called except on birthdays and festivals! Fiza called her maybe once in a month, and the call hardly lasted for two minutes.

With a feeling of trepidation, she took the call and sat down on her bed to talk. All about being late for work was forgotten!

The rage on *khala's* face said it all. She knew that her worst nightmare had come true. *khala* had come to know about everything that was going on! This was the last thing she wanted—*Khala* getting to know through the media. She had planned to inform her about the wedding and have the wedding in London or India. If she wished to come, she could, otherwise Fiza was prepared to have a wedding only in the presence of friends.

She did not want to cause *khala* any trouble. She had done so much for her, and even though she never said it in so many words, it was a truth that always hung in the air between them.

Khala did not say anything but put the camera of the phone on the newspaper that she was carrying in her hands. The headlines read, "The daughter of the foreign secretary wants India and Pakistan to unite at the 100th year of partition."

There was her picture, taken in one of the concerts that she had attended when she was in Islamabad, which showed her face very clearly. It also had *khala's* picture on the left with a caption beneath: "Does our foreign secretary also support this crazy idea?"

Then *khala* came on the line. She looked furious. Her face was red, and she was short of breath. Usually a woman of few words, her tongue would not stop when she was angry. Today, she had a lot to say.

"Years ago, when I gave shelter to a young girl of eight, I thought I was providing for my old age; a daughter who would take care of me. Little did I know that I was bringing up a snake who would grow up to bite me. It was my mistake. There were people who had advised me not to adopt from a lower class, but I wouldn't listen. They were right. After everything that I did for you, you have just destroyed my career, my life.

"I worked hard and somehow made a life for myself when he divorced me. I earned money, respect and fame. I managed to pick up the pieces of my shattered life when he left. And today, you have succeeded in accomplishing the mission in which he had failed — ruining me completely."

Fiza was shocked. She wanted to explain, but she could not utter a word.

Khala continued, "I did not agree with your lifestyle, but did I ever say anything? I let you have your life in London. What did I expect from you? Just that whenever you came home, you would behave as is expected of the daughter of a foreign secretary. If you wanted to marry an Indian boy, you could have done so and stayed away from here! Why all this fuss? And anyway, why do you want to marry a madman?"

Never in all her life had Fiza seen *khala* so angry. Not even when her political rivals had framed her in a false case and initiated a departmental enquiry against her.

"Blood is thicker than water, but you are not my blood." Her last sentence felt like a barb, and Fiza felt a physical pain pierce through her heart.

Khala disconnected the call, and Fiza kept sitting on the bed with her head in her hands. Her heart felt as if it could burst. She wanted to scream her lungs out. She wanted to let the pain out. If only she had a time machine, she would go back in time and ignore Karan's advances when they had met at that ghazal concert. She would never start a story which would destroy everyone and everything around it.

She sat there like a zombie. The phone rang again, and she looked at the screen to see who was calling. This time, it was Mehrunisa *aapa*. She was her *khala's* personal secretary. She was perhaps the person *khala* was closest to. Fiza talked to her more than she talked to *khala*. What *khala* lacked in communication, Mehrunisa more than made up for with her way with words.

Fiza knew that she was calling up to say things which *khala* would not say herself. She was her spokesperson. She also did all her dirty work.

Fiza took the call even though she was in no mood to talk to anyone.

"As-Salaam-Alaikum *aapa*," she said.

"*Wa –alaikum -salaam*" came the reply from the other side.

"What is happening, beta? When did you get involved in all this? I am sure you have become a victim of some malicious political game which our opponents are playing. Everyone knows that your *Khala* is very close to the Prime Minister, and hence, people are trying to malign her name to ensure his downfall. Had it been only her who was affected, she would still not have minded perhaps, but when it comes to our Prime Minister, she can't take any chance."

"*Aapa*, I don't know how it got out of hand, but I will try to set things right," Fiza somehow managed to reply.

"Nothing you say or do now is going to help matters. They will dig further and come out with more filth, some real and some imaginary. There is only one way out. You come home and get married. That will settle all the rumors," she said as a matter of fact.

For a moment, the world felt dark. She was unable to comprehend or say anything. She wanted to disconnect the call but was unable to do even that. She was in a trance-like situation. What was *Aapa* saying? She should go to

Islamabad and get married to some unknown person? She must be out of her mind to even suggest this.

But she knew it was not *Aapa* but her *Khala* speaking through her. So, this is what she wanted – for her to get married in Islamabad to prove everyone wrong.

Aapa kept on saying something; not much of it got registered in Fiza's mind though. *Aapa* finally kept the phone down after telling her that she would be sending tickets for her travel after some time.

Fiza kept the phone down and sank to the floor. With her head on her knees, arms hugging her legs, she started to scream.

NEW DELHI

Karan was furious, and he left a positively upset Anu alone in the restaurant. Though he did not raise his voice even a notch, he was fuming from inside. Why could she not understand one simple thing, that this could not be political. If he had wanted to join politics, he could have joined when he was in college. Moreover, he had been very clear with Anu, if not with others, about his other reason for not making it political.

He needed to think. He always thought well when he was walking, and so, he went to Lodhi Garden for a walk. He really needed to finish this thing fast. Once the march to Islamabad was done and he was able to convey what he wanted to convey, he would leave everything and go back to London to be with Fiza. The seed, after it was sown, would bear fruit, sooner or later. He wanted to sow the seed, not eat the fruit.

Why did Anu not understand this simple thing? If she wanted to join Ekta Party, she was free to do so herself. He would never stop her! Why was she after him to join it?

Moreover, he did not like the way she tried to suggest that there was something more than friendship between them. She knew how much he loved Fiza. Why did she then give him a feeling that she wanted to be more than friends with him?

Karan was really agitated as he walked. Thoughts were crashing upon his mind like waves, one after the other. It was then that his phone rang. It was an unidentified number. These days, he was getting a lot of calls from people wanting to join the movement or the march.

Absentmindedly, he took the call.

"I am Sooraj. We have never met, but Anu must have told you about me," the person on the line started without exchanging any pleasantries. "I came to know that you have declined the offer to join Ekta Party. That made me think that you have some sense in you. Now I hear that you are talking about some public peace march from Delhi to Islamabad!"

"Yes, your information is correct, but then we have already announced it in front of the media so it's not a big secret," Karan snapped.

"Don't you dare act superior! I know your type. In the garb of being apolitical, you all have an axe to grind. Whatever it is that you stand to gain from this movement, I will tell you one thing. You will not achieve anything from this movement because I will not let it happen." Sooraj was speaking in the same tone without raising his voice. "You people come from abroad and try to preach about peace. If you cared so much, why did you leave the country? Stay here and fight the battles," he said.

Karan sat down on the nearest bench. This will take some time, he thought.

Sooraj continued, "Look here, we have toiled hard, night and day to unite and convince the Hindus to fight for their rights. All this peace talk you are doing is not helping matters. Please understand, peace can only prevail when people on both sides start with a clean slate. This can never be the case with us. We are carrying the weight of 100 years of history on our shoulders. We are burdened with a past which is bloody and full of treachery and betrayal."

"I agree with what you are saying, but the wounds of the past need to be healed with doses of love," Karan interrupted.

"Bullshit! That's not possible. We have drifted apart, and no amount of love and friendship can ever bridge the gap." This time Sooraj raised his voice. "Look here, I have devoted my youth to this cause, to my Hindu Maha Morcha. Elections are around the corner, and I will not allow a crazy NRI to come like a hurricane and blow away all my dreams." Sooraj was again in control and sounded as if he was weighing every word before speaking.

"I don't agree with you that it's too late for love and friendship to be given a chance in this case. In fact, I am talking about the union of the two nations." Karan was prepared for mocking laughter from the other end, but Sooraj cut him off abruptly.

"I am not interested in knowing about your pipe dreams, nor am I here to convince you. I am just telling you to leave all this nonsense and go back to where you have come from. Just leave! It will be good for you and your family! If you continue with your work here, I promise you that you will not be going back anywhere ever! I don't make false promises. Ask Anu, she will tell you."

"Are you threatening me?" Karan was now agitated.

"I don't threaten, I promise," Sooraj said in a sinister voice.

What was happening? A little while ago Anu was pressurizing him. Now this goon was threatening him! 'What is happening?' Karan thought.

He was already on the edge when he walked out of the restaurant, leaving a shocked Anu behind. Now this call was the final straw.

He felt a rage building inside him and flowing through his throbbing veins. Enough was enough!

"Look here, whoever you are, and I don't need anyone to tell me that you are just a goon! Let me make this very clear. No one is going to bulldoze me into doing or not doing anything. I will do whatever I feel like, and you can do whatever you want. You have chosen the wrong person to threaten. Just because I am talking of peace does not mean that I can't handle some hard-shelled nitwits. I am man enough to challenge you to try and stop me. Go to hell and don't call me again!" Karan was shivering in anger when he disconnected the call.

He put the phone inside his pocket and rested his head on the backrest of the bench. He closed his eyes and took a deep breath. So much was happening so quickly! Where was the Karan who was drifting aimlessly in life; the vagabond cloud floating in the sky? He now felt as if he was carrying a huge burden. He felt as if he was the Atlas, and the world rested on his shoulders! Ah, the only soothing thought in his life was that of Fiza. Thinking of her, a smile broke out on his face, even though he was so agitated. She always had this effect on him. How he loved her! 'I can forsake the entire world for her,' he thought.

The phone rang again. It was Fiza. He felt a gush of emotion in his heart and wanted to reach out to her and crush her in his arms. He wanted to bury his head in her hair and forget all about India and Pakistan. All he wanted to remember was their love. He felt his eyes go misty, and his voice was muffled as he took the call.

"I was thinking of you," he said as he looked at a visibly upset Fiza on the phone screen. She was in her room and her eyes were red. She had been crying!

"What happened?" He asked. Nothing was going right since morning, and he felt a strange sensation of foreboding.

"Karan, you promised me that my name and identity would not come out in the media. You broke your promise. I am now breaking my promise to marry you. I am sorry," she said.

Karan felt a pain so fierce in his heart that for a moment he felt like he was having a heart attack. He wished he actually had one. Anything was better than this! He tried to open his mouth and say something, but no words came out of his mouth.

He could not breathe, he could not speak, and he just froze at her words.

"You have nothing to say?" Fiza asked. Even though her eyes were red, she was now calm.

Karan tried to speak but no words came out of his mouth. He simply shook his head.

"Okay, then. Some relationships are just not meant to be. I am sorry." she said as she disconnected the call.

The pain in his heart was getting worse. He pressed his hand against his chest and bent down. His head resting on his knees, he sat there feeling dazed. The pain, no, it was no longer pain, it was a ghastly heaviness in his heart that was pulling him down. He had to throw out whatever was weighing on his chest. He had to do something! He raised his head and closed his ears with both his hands. Then he screamed. He screamed till his breath fell short. He screamed till he was panting. Since it was early evening, not many people were walking in the park. The few who were there looked at him and then carried on with their walk. They perhaps thought that he was a mad person.

One elderly lady though, took a chance and came to him.

"Are you all right, *beta?*" She asked. Her words brought him back from whichever plane he had travelled to in the past few minutes. He looked startled, but he tried to compose himself.

"I am not fine, but I will be all right. Thank you, aunty," he said.

Then he took out his phone to call Vivek, for he was in no position to drive back home.

NEWHAM, LONDON

The dreaded call was over! The shock on his face had been so obvious. He had been jolted too hard to react to what she had said.

Fiza did not want to break down when she was speaking to Karan. She did not. The moment that she disconnected the call, the dam burst. She cried for the love that she had lost. She cried for the happiness that was within her grasp only to elude her in the end. She cried for the hurt and humiliation she had caused to the only family she had. She cried for the family she had just lost. She cried for the mother she vaguely remembered. She cried for all the times she had put up a brave front. She cried for the past; she cried for the future. It was as if the river Thames had found an outlet through her eyes — the tears just kept flowing.

Felicia was quiet, for she was not programmed to deal with her sobbing. Everything was still in the room; only the bed shook with her sobs.

She lay down there for hours. The evening sky was blushing a crimson red, and the shadows were creeping on into the room. They had already found a place in her heart.

It was another call which broke her reverie. This time, it was *khala's* secretary again, telling her that her return ticket was booked for the next day. She told Fiza that she need not worry about packing anything and just had to bring the bare minimum. The rest of her stuff and her flat would be taken care of by someone else later.

How ironic, a home that took years to build, became just another 'flat' in a matter of minutes!

Fiza listened to whatever she said without any argument. She knew it was futile to fight. These people would go to any lengths to get what they wanted. She had neither the time, nor the energy to fight anyone. She knew that she could not marry Karan now, but she was also very sure that she would not marry anyone else. This she would have to explain to them in person.

She did call up her few friends to say goodbye. She just told them that she was going home due to some family emergency.

She then got up to pack a few of her clothes and stuff. The first suit that she took was the peacock blue *anarkali* suit that Karan had gifted her. She still remembered the day she had fought with him on some issue and had been sulking. Karan had left her flat in anger. It was after an hour or so that he had returned with a cake and this beautiful suit, saying, "Let's celebrate our first fight." He had lifted her off the bed in his arms and made her change. They had cut the cake and made passionate love on the carpet.

The memory brought another bout of tears. Her life in the past year had become entwined with his. There was no memory of which he was not a part. It was not possible to tear apart a page from your past and discard it so easily.

This is why she had never wanted to get close to people. It always ended in pain. There was no point in regretting anything now, though. She was under a moral obligation to see to it that her aunt and her political career were not harmed in any way. Karan had gone on to take up such a big challenge just to please his father. She too owed this much to her aunt. She would have to go back and do whatever her aunt asked to make amends, even if it meant breaking off all ties with Karan.

That night, she could not sleep at all. There was a call from Vivek which she did not answer. After some time, there was a call from Karan, and she did not know what else she could say to him. He would obviously try to persuade her to change her mind, so she switched off her phone.

Next day, when she landed in Islamabad airport, *aapa* was there to receive her.

"Fiza, when will you stop getting into trouble? You were sent to London so that you could live the life that you wanted, and your *khala* could live here without worrying about what damage you would do to her reputation. Look what you have done now!" The disapproval was writ all over her face. Her lips were smiling, but her eyes were cold.

Fiza kept quiet. She did not want to get into an argument. Moreover, what could she say? The arrangement had been very clear between them. She could live her life the way she wanted to as long as *khala*'s name did not get dragged into any controversy due to her actions. She had broken the arrangement, and now, she had to do whatever they wanted.

As the car sped through the city, Fiza reminisced her earlier life here. The memories were not very pleasant. Her childhood, for obvious reasons, had been very subdued. They entered her *khala*'s home, the beautiful bungalow where she had spent her childhood. There was a big, beautifully maintained garden. It had a small pond in the middle with lotus flowers. She remembered running after the butterflies in this very garden. There were some pleasant memories too!

Khala was waiting on the sofa without a smile on her face. She nodded when she looked at Fiza. She was meeting Fiza after more than three years, and this was how she received her! Of course, circumstances were not congenial.

Fiza greeted her and sat down on the sofa next to her. Without any pleasantries, *khala* began, "I need not mention how much damage the news has already done to my reputation. Now we have to settle things, and I expect you to cooperate with us. We will have a press conference where you will deny all the rumors, and then, in a day or two we will announce your engagement with Parvez Miyan."

Fiza felt the ground slip beneath her feet! Marry Parvez? *Khala* must be out of her mind to suggest this!

Parvez was a distant cousin whom she had never liked even as a child. He was a doctor, though she always wondered how he had become one. Some five or six years elder to her, he was a rogue. He used to find ways to trouble her, sometimes by pulling her braid, sometimes intimidating her by looking at her fiercely. As a child she had been scared, and as an adult, she was repulsed.

"*Khala*, I have broken off with Karan, but I will not marry anyone. I will live the way you tell me, will do whatever you want, but I will not marry anyone" Fiza's reply was laced with panic.

"You will now do whatever we say. London was where you were supposed to live as you wanted. This is Islamabad, and here you live as my daughter, a daughter who has always been ungrateful for all that I did for her. If I had not adopted you, you would have been married to a man your father's age and would have been a mother of teenaged kids by now. That too only if you had survived hunger and poverty to reach adulthood in the first place. Instead of being grateful, you have constantly been a source of trouble for me. Forget everything about freedom. Here, you do what I say, and that is final." *Khala*'s words sounded like a death sentence to Fiza.

Perhaps, if she had known this, she would not have come. She would have disappeared somewhere in the big world.

She suddenly realized that she had actually walked into a prison. She had lost her free will, her identity, the moment she had entered her *khala*'s house. She was a prisoner!

NEW DELHI

It had just been a couple of days, but it felt like forever! Every moment was torture. "Why do we attach ourselves to someone so much that separation feels like death", wondered Karan. He had never in his wildest dreams thought that they would not be together! Marriage or no marriage, they were meant to be together.

Fiza had always mentioned how indebted to her *khala* she was and also, how *khala* had never let her forget this fact. That she had so much control over her and her life, he had not realized. He felt an excruciating pain in his chest, and he knew it was not a symptom of a heart attack but heartbreak itself. He had not eaten properly in two days. He had not slept, not shaved, not spoken to anyone except Vivek and Anu. He had moved to Anu's room because he did not want his family to see what he was going through. He couldn't stay with Vivek as he stayed with his parents, whereas Anu lived alone.

Both Vivek and Anu were constantly by his side. Vivek had never seen his childhood friend in this condition before! He looked completely shattered! 'If this is what love does to people, I would not want to fall in love ever,' Vivek thought to himself.

What they were not able to understand was how the information had been leaked. Even in London, hardly anyone knew of her connection to her aunt. They racked their brains but could not find an answer.

Meanwhile, the media in India also exploited the news – "Mystery Girl Revealed," "Mystery Girl from Pakistan's Political Circles," and "The Daughter of a close aide to the Pakistan Prime Minister is behind the movement to unite India and Pakistan." All tabloids and news channels were adding lot of imagination to the story, the details of which were not completely known to anyone. They just knew the lead characters, but this did not stop them from weaving their own fairytales!

Courtesy the leak, their movement had become the headline news again, and every day, more people were joining them. It was growing exponentially and was becoming difficult to manage.

This was not a time when they could afford to lose even a couple of hours, but they had already lost a couple of days!

At the back of his mind, Karan was aware that he had gone so much ahead with the entire plan that it was next to impossible to call it off. His announcement of the march, from Delhi to Islamabad, had set the ball rolling, and it would not stop on its own.

Anu had been explaining this to him continuously, not that he needed to understand. He understood it all right. Only, he did not feel like doing anything, now that Fiza had gone from his life. Fiza had switched off her phone. He contacted Riyaz, who in turn tried to contact her, but her whereabouts were not known. She had simply disappeared from public eye.

Feeling helpless and distraught, Karan wished he had not started this at all! "All this drama, for what purpose?" He asked his friends.

It was then that Anu lost her cool.

"Was the entire movement just about getting one girl? Where are your ideals, your values now? All that talk about uniting the two countries, was that a sham? The ostentatious idea of the union of the two countries was all just an eyewash? What about the thousands of people who have joined us, shown their faith in us? What about thousands of mothers who are hoping for a day when they will not have to lose their sons to wars? What about the millions of people in the world who are watching us, waiting for us to create history?" Anu's face turned red as she spoke angrily. A part of her was jealous that he was so much in love with Fiza that he wanted to forsake everything. The other part was furious that months of hard work and commitment were going to go waste because of a mere girl! She would have none of it!

"Get up now!" She commanded in a voice that even Karan could not ignore. He got up from the bed and just stared at her. Vivek was also looking at her in awe. He had not seen her like this ever.

"This is the last time I am hearing this girl's name. No one will talk about her now." She looked at Karan and said, "It must be hurting really bad. It always does, but it gets better."

Her voice became gentle now. She came and hugged Karan. Karan started weeping. His body shivered as he sobbed.

"Make your pain your strength. It will give you power. Earlier, you were fighting for your own personal agenda, now you will fight for the society, for the betterment of people. You are not an ordinary man, Karan. You have not started a movement, my friend, you have started a revolution. Wear your pain like a medallion and be proud of it." She kept running her fingers through his hair and at the same time rocked him like a baby as he cried his heart out for the girl he had loved and had lost.

ISLAMABAD

In just a couple of days, Fiza realized that she had made a grave mistake by listening to her *aapa* and her *khala* On the second day of her arrival, a small press conference was called, in which her *khala* had declared all the news that was being shown as baseless and a malicious design of the opposition party and that Fiza was engaged to her cousin. Fiza forced herself to smile through the charade. A couple of journalists insisted on getting a reply from Fiza directly to which she said what she had been instructed to, "I just knew this man in London, and he was a friend. He was nothing more and will never be anything more than a friend. All this talk about him proposing to reunite India and Pakistan is utterly false. If he is doing that, he must have political aspirations, and I have no part to play in it." Fiza had never felt like such a hypocrite in her life!

Khala employed a middle-aged lady, whose sole purpose was to keep an eye on Fiza. Her name was Farzana, and she looked like a character straight out of horror movies. She had only one eye. The other eye was made of glass. An obscure nose and thin lips only succeeded in drawing even more attention to the false eye and frizzy boy-cut hair. Overall, more than the looks, it was the death cold eye and the unforgiving sinister look that made her look creepy.

Farzana never left Fiza alone even for a moment. Even when she was in the bathroom, she would be outside the door, knocking after every five minutes to check on her. It was so irritating and frustrating!

The other day, she was forced to go on a dinner date with Parvez. She was to be seen in public with him. This was all part of the plan. During the dinner, as they spoke a little, Fiza was aghast at how anyone could be so regressive in his thinking in 2047! Parvez believed that the cause of all the evils in the world was the sexual desire of women. This made a woman do things which were against her nature. Allah had made her for pleasing men and for raising children, but when she had started thinking of the 'self', the entire problem had started. He believed that the *'khatna'* of women was a good practice which kept the women's desire under control and the society pure! Fiza was aghast! He was even more a monster than she remembered!

"You have a lot to learn," he said, "and I will enjoy teaching you. I never liked the insolent look you had, even as a child. I always wanted to break you like a horse and tame you. I am happy that finally I will be doing that," he said with a menacing look in his eyes, even though his lips were smiling. It sent a chill down her spine. She averted his eyes and kept quiet. She knew that her reaction would do her more harm than good. *Khala* and everyone else should be made to believe that she was truly repentant of all that had happened and was now doing what was asked of her. She needed to buy some time and find a way to escape! She had to think of something before it was too late!

She had tried reasoning with *khala*, promising her that she would return to London and sever all ties with Karan. Khala was unmoved. Fiza was aware of that fact that her Khala had never loved her, but now, for some reason, she hated her.

She was trapped in her own house and held prisoner by her own adoptive mother! She had no access to the phone. She was not allowed to meet anyone. Who would have believed that this was possible in these modern times! In Pakistan, everything was possible! Once, she had even managed to get out of the house and reach the main gate. However, the security guards did not open the main gate and informed *khala*. Khala told the guards in front of her, "If she tries to escape again, you have the authority to pull the trigger. She should not go out of the house alive under any condition."

They fixed her *nikah* for the 15th of August 2047, the day Karan was to start his march for peace. She needed to do something quickly!

Mustafa saw her sitting on the sofa, next to the Chinese vase, deep in her thoughts. She looked sad, like always. The only difference was that today, that horrible-looking woman was not with her. This was an opportunity. He could not let it pass.

Mustafa was the son of the lady who delivered flowers to *khala's* residence. One day, his mother had felt unwell and had asked him to deliver the flowers. That was the day he had seen her crying alone, sitting on a bench near the lotus pond. Next day, he volunteered to deliver flowers in this area, saying that it was near to his college. There was something fishy here, he knew it. He was made to deposit his phone to the guard at the main gate before entering the house. The horrible-looking lady was always hovering around her.

His job was to replace all the flowers in the vase with fresh flowers. He went to her and extended his hands to show the fresh bunch of flowers that he had got.

"*Aapa*, today I have got some special flowers. They are the first dahlia of the season, bright and colorful like you," he blushed as he inadvertently gave his secret away. The infatuation that a teenage boy has for a beautiful lady was clearly visible in his eyes. It was not missed by Fiza either.

"What's your name?" She asked him.

"Mustafa," he replied. He had not expected anything more than a nod from her. He suddenly found himself tongue-tied. She glanced at the door of the living room as if to check if that lady was watching them. On seeing that she was not present, she hesitatingly asked him, "Mustafa, I need your help. Will you help me?"

Mustafa simply nodded in reply. He wanted to tell her that he knew she was in trouble and that he would do anything to help her, but no words came out of his mouth.

"I will write everything and keep it in the vase. You please read it and act accordingly. You will have to be very careful and not let anyone know about this. Can you do this?"

"Your flowers are not looking fresh," she told him, and he was taken aback by this sudden change of topic before realizing the presence of that dragon lady behind him.

"Run off now. Don't hang around here, and also get fresh flowers tomorrow, not stale ones," the dragon lady said, dismissing him.

Mustafa ran out of the house, his heart beating faster. So, his hunch had been correct after all. She was indeed a prisoner in her house.

That evening, he asked his ammi about her, and she told him that there was a rumor that she was in love with an Indian man who was talking about uniting Pakistan with India. The rumors were laid to rest when it was announced that she would be marrying her cousin.

Now, Mustafa could somewhat understand what the problem was, but how could he help her, he wondered.

The next day, he was there on time with the flowers. She was nowhere to be seen, but the dragon lady was there. He got to work, taking out the bouquet of fresh chrysanthemums from his bag and laying them by the side of the vase. He then took out the wilted flowers from the vase. As he did that, his fingers went deep into the vase and encountered a small plastic pouch. He quickly put that pouch in his bag along with the old flowers. After arranging the fresh flowers, he quietly went out of the room. It was only when he was safely out of the house that he took out the pouch. Inside was a letter, as she had said. It was written in Urdu in a beautiful handwriting.

With his heart beating fast, he read the letter, and after reading it, he kept it safely inside the pocket of his *kurta*. He will help this lovely lady. Everything happens for a purpose, his mother always said. His mother had fallen sick because he was destined to meet Fiza and help her. That was Allah's will. 'I will not fail her,' Mustafa thought as he took out the letter again and read it, with the same concentration as before.

NEW DELHI

Anu was sitting by the side of the hospital bed on which Karan lay. He was running a very high temperature, so they had to bring him to the hospital. He was better today. Vivek had just gone out of the room to see off Karan's family. Both his father and uncle insisted that they would stay with him in the hospital, but the doctor firmly declined. They had no option but to leave.

Anu was also about to leave when there was a beep on her phone. It was a personal message on the social handle of their group. They got many messages, more so because people got to know that Karan was not well.

She absentmindedly opened the message, and the moment she read it, she froze. She sat still for some time and re-read the message.

Just then, Karan opened his eyes. "I want to talk to Fiza," he said. "Please give me my phone." She knew that if he saw the message on their social handle it would be catastrophic. She had to decide fast. She would not let one stupid Pakistani girl ruin all that they had worked for, with reckless behavior. She handed over her own phone to him after dialing Fiza's number.

Like always, it was switched off. Anu now knew why it was switched off! It was all in the message that came just now from an unknown account. She was a prisoner in her own house, about to get married to her cousin on 15th August. She had requested Karan to leak this information to the media so that she could be rescued. She had apologized for breaking up with him and professed her love for him.

It was torturous to see the agony on Karan's face as he kept the phone aside. It was for his own good though, she thought. We often have to take bitter medicines to get well. The gold has to burn in the furnace to be shaped into a beautiful ornament. The same way, he will would have to endure this pain as he was destined to do much greater things in life. He had to move on. Time would heal his wounds and things would get better, she knew. She would make it better. She had made up her mind, and when she did this, nothing could stop her.

Sitting by his side, she reminded him of the things to be done before the march. The clearances to be taken, the legal formalities to be completed, the venue of the speech to be decided and also the letter that they would be giving to the prime ministers of the two countries, to be drafted. The list was endless.

Karan got distracted by the pending work, and this was very much the plan. They started discussing and planning about the important events that lay ahead of them. By now, Vivek had also joined them.

"Once this march is over, I will go back to London," Karan said suddenly, in the middle of the important discussion that they were having.

"Ok, you do whatever you want. First, let it get over," Vivek said.

Anu just nodded at them with a faraway look on her face as she brought the discussion back to the topic again.

Things were falling into place. She just needed some patience. They could not afford to lose Karan. He was the magnet that pulled people to their movement in large numbers. The sincerity in his speeches, and the honest eyes never failed to convince people. Moreover, when he said that he had no political ambitions, people believed him. He had no political background or motivation.

This break-up with his girlfriend, though good for them, was pulling them behind their schedule. He had to get out of this '*Devdas* mode' soon.

Anu read the message again. For a moment, she felt sorry for the girl. An educated, smart and independent girl being held captive! Then she reminded herself that Karan was much better off without her. She would be a liability to their cause. With a determined look on her face, she selected the message and pressed the delete button.

ISLAMABAD

The flower boy was her only hope, and she wondered if he would be able to understand what she had written, and even if he did, if he would be willing to help her.

She had asked him to send a message to the social handle of the group. She had conveyed that she was being held captive and that she needed this to be out in the media so that her aunt was forced to release her.

Mustafa had gestured to her that he had done her job, but even then, there was no change in the situation. Was it possible that no one had read the message? Though, it was unlikely that this could have happened. She was at her wit's end as to how to deal with the situation.

Her aunt would meet her every day for dinner and would maintain a stoic silence. Every time that Fiza requested her to allow her to go to London, she would start talking about how Fiza had betrayed her trust and how she had to suffer political backlash because of her behavior. She would again remind her that she would have been living a life of utmost poverty in some slum if she had not adopted her. She would then tell her that she would be given her freedom only after her marriage to Parvez.

Farzana, on the other hand, would never utter a word to her, but she would look at her with such contempt that if looks could kill, she would be dead by now.

If someone had told her a month back that she would be a prisoner, she would have scoffed at them. What was highly improbable and unlikely had actually happened! She regretted her decision of trusting *khala*! She knew that all that she cared for was her political career, and she had no real love for Fiza. She did not have a single motherly bone in her body.

She would have to get out of here soon. But how?

She was mulling over this dilemma when suddenly, she remembered a person she knew would be able to help her. A smile lit up her face just like the sun lights up the sky, peeping from behind the dark clouds. Jawed was a distant cousin. He was nearly ten years her senior. He and *khala* could not stand each other. He was an active member of a party that was in opposition to *khala*'s party. Whenever they met, sparks would fly. No one dared to speak to her the way Jawed *bhai jaan* did.

His thought evoked many memories. Fiza remembered the day when he had had a heated argument with *khala* in the living room, while she was sitting on the porch, from where she could hear them clearly. They had been shouting at and abusing each other, and she had sat there terrified. When he came out of the house and saw little Fiza huddled in the corner of the porch, scared and in tears, he had sat down beside her. Putting his arms around her, he had wiped her tears and said, "I really pity you for having such a person as your mother. She is not human; she is a selfish beast who is only interested in her career. You should get away from her as soon as possible." Then, patting her head again, he had left.

After this incident, every time they met in some family gathering, there would be an unspoken camaraderie between them. One day, when they were alone, he had told her if ever she needed any help, she should come to him.

Thinking of Jawed brought a spurt of energy in Fiza. Why had she not thought of him earlier? After going to London, she had lost touch with most of the people back home. Jawed *bhai jaan* had become a journalist and was running a channel. He would always target *khala*'s party. She knew he would gladly help her.

She immediately wrote a letter to Jawed *bhai* and a note to Mustafa. She instructed him to go the office of the news channel and personally hand over her letter to Jawed. It was not an easy task, but she hoped that he would be able to do it.

She then put both the letters in a plastic pouch and slipped them inside the vase. Now, the only thing she could do was to wait for Mustafa.

Mustafa came at his usual time, and she indicated with her eye movement that there was something in the vase. From the corner of her eyes, she saw him put his fingers inside the vase and pull out the pouch. He quietly sneaked it into his pocket. Fiza breathed a sigh of relief and fervently prayed that the letter somehow reached Jawed *bhai*. He would find a way to rescue her, she was sure.

She had not been sleeping well since the day she had arrived. She would be tossing and turning in her bed most of the night. But previous night, she had not slept a wink. She knew this was her last chance.

It was around 9 a.m. in the morning when she heard a lot of commotion in the house and realized something was happening. Farzana came to her room with the breakfast tray and told her to stay indoors. She then locked her room from outside!

Something was brewing. She was at the edge not knowing what was happening and hoping that whatever was happening was in her favour.

The whole day, she stayed in the room without food. It was around 3 p.m. in the afternoon that the door opened, and she saw Jawed standing there. She ran into his arms and broke down.

"Let's go," he said. "I have all your papers." She searched for *khala,* who was nowhere to be seen. Farzana was standing there, looking livid.

"How did you manage to communicate with him?" She asked. Fiza ignored her question, hoping they never found out that Mustafa had helped her.

They walked towards the main gate, and all the while, she was scared that any moment they would be hit by a bullet, but Jawed seemed relaxed. When she walked out of the gate and sat in the car that was waiting for them, she could finally breathe! Free at last! Never in her life would she have dreamt that she would be held a prisoner, that too in her own house. Freedom was so precious, so valuable, she realized at that moment. We don't value what we have until it is taken away!

On the way to Jawed bhai jaan's house, he told her what had happened. Jawed had been out of the country when all this had happened. He had returned only a couple of days back.

The previous day, in the afternoon, in the office, he was told that someone wanted to meet him to hand over a letter personally. When asked about the reason or agenda, he had only said it was very important, and it was a matter of life and death for someone close to Jawed. So, of course, he met him and realized who it was!

"All that is okay but how did you convince *khala?*" She asked.

"Do you think that woman can be convinced? No, people like her can only be manipulated. That is the only language they understand," disgust was written on his face.

"I have dug out something which she wants to keep a secret. Many years back, she had an affair with one of the ministers. I had some pictures of them together. I was saving them for the day when she would come for me, trying to implicate me in some false case. That did not happen, because she knew she was better off without rousing my wrath." He was smiling now, enjoying his victory.

"She gave in easily, without causing a ruckus?" Fiza was still scared that *khala* would not accept defeat that easily.

"No, I had to promise her that you would not talk about all this to anyone, especially the media. She would rather be known as a mother whose daughter rebelled against her than a mother who held her daughter as a captive!"

"Now what, *bhai jaan?*" She was suddenly scared again. All this was happening so quickly and so unexpectedly that it felt bizarre.

"Now, you tell me everything from the beginning," he said, taking her hands in his and giving it a tight squeeze. He could still see the traces of an eleven-year-old terrified girl crying on the porch.

Fiza leaned back against her seat and closed her eyes. She never knew that a simple thing like having someone to talk to was so important in life. She wanted to pour her heart out; she wanted to share her pain, her anguish and her fears. All she needed now was a shoulder to rest her head on and a sympathetic pair of ears. She was used to talking to Felicia whenever she was alone and felt the need for company. All the same, no machine can ever replace the warmth of a human touch.

Then she started telling the story from the beginning from where it had all begun – Chandni Chowk, India, in the year 2030.

NEW DELHI

She was flying, literally and figuratively. She was on a flight to New Delhi. It was only a couple of days since she had been rescued, but it felt like a century. Every minute away from Karan now felt like an eternity. She was dying to meet Karan. After staying away from him, she now had no doubts that she wanted to live her life with this man.

She had broken up with Karan only in a moment of rage. But the feeling of anguish towards him would have subsided with time, and she would have patched up with him by now if she had the time. But she had been taken a prisoner! She was now sure as death that she wanted to spend the rest of her life with Karan, marriage or no marriage.

Jawed was very impressed by the idea Karan was propagating. "The idea in entirety is not practical, but things could be worked out to bring more peace and brotherhood between the two nations," he said. He offered to align with the movement and take it further on Pakistan soil.

He had given his blessings to her decision and had promised her that he would be attending her wedding from her side and would even do the fatherly rituals for the bride, if required. Fiza had smiled at this. She was not sure if there would be a marriage at all. Marriage would happen only if Karan's father agreed to it.

She was also clear in her mind that she would convince Karan to withdraw from all the mass movements that he had started, hand over the command to someone else, most probably Anu and go back to London with her. They had had enough of it! It had almost separated them! Now, all she wanted was to take her man and live her life! It did not matter where, but she wanted nothing to do with politics or public attention.

Jawed had suggested that they should try to get in touch with Karan, but Fiza had a different idea. She wanted to see the happiness on his face when he saw her. She wanted to surprise him, and so, they had decided that she would fly to Delhi and would go meet him at his office.

The flight was short, but every moment seemed like an eternity. She closed her eyes and allowed herself to go down the memory lane.

She remembered an incident when, after a bad day at work, she had returned home in a foul mood. She had fought with him for no reason and was sulking on her bed when the lights were suddenly switched off, and for a moment everything was in darkness. The next moment, the room was filled with yellow, fluorescent halogen smiley balloons that glowed in the dark! She could not help but smile back.

On her birthday, Karan had booked a table in the sky restaurant, where she had cut a cake hanging hundreds of feet above the ground, in the air!

Karan was not only an old-fashioned romantic, he was also a very caring, sensitive and a good human being.

On Eid, he had arranged a visit to a nearby state-run orphanage where he had sponsored a full meal for the children.

It is true that you only realize the true worth of a person when you lose them. Well, she had almost lost him!

As the plane touched down at the Indira Gandhi International Airport, she was reminded of the young girl who had landed on the same soil some 17 years ago, full of curiosity and exhilaration.

Today too, she felt like a teenager and was almost bursting with anticipation. She booked a cab, and soon she was in the streets of Delhi, racing through the buzzing streets and past multi-storied buildings.

Oh, Delhi had changed! If she had not known, she could not have made out the difference between New York and Delhi. Indians had made remarkable progress in infrastructure, it seemed. No wonder that they were one of the superpowers of the world today. Pakistan, on the other hand, had a long way to go.

The cab stopped at the building which housed the office of the 'Unite for Peace' movement. She hurriedly alighted from the cab and walked towards the building. With her heart beating so hard that she could actually hear it, she opened the door and walked in.

The first thing that caught her eye was a painting on the wall. It was a map of India and Pakistan without the border dividing them. The caption below it read, 'Unite for Peace.'

The office was a hub of activity. Many people were busy working at their workstations, and many others were having discussions in groups. They were mainly youngsters. There was a boy with blue hair who was sitting in front of his system, busy designing something. Fiza went to him and asked, "Is Karan in?" And as she waited with bated breath, he casually nodded and pointed towards a room to his right.

The room had a nameplate, and on it was written artistically in a beautiful, cursive hand, 'Karan.'

With trembling hands, she opened the door and walked inside.

There he was! Sitting on a chair facing the wall on which a presentation was being projected. A girl, probably Anu, was standing beside him, her right hand on his shoulders while her left hand was pointing at the presentation, trying to make some point.

Before she could say anything, he turned and looked at her, blinking his eyes as if to ascertain that he was not daydreaming.

"Fiza…" he cried out as she ran into his arms.

"Is it you, my darling? Is it really you? I knew you would come back. I knew you cannot stay without me? Why did you not answer my calls?" He was blabbering and crying at the same time.

Fiza too was sobbing as she gently put her fingers on his lips. "Hush, later, for now, just hold me in your arms," she said.

As the presentation kept on playing on the screen and two lovers remained entwined, sobbing and laughing at the same time, Anu quietly made an exit from the room, shutting the door behind her.

A few hours later, they lay spent and exhausted on the bed at Anu's house. Since her house was near, they had taken the keys from her and had gone there.

After making frantic, wild and passionate love in which they devoured each other as if there was no tomorrow, they again made tender love, worshipping, caressing each other's bodies as if there was no other thing in the world that was as important as their lovemaking. Every touch, every whisper, every sigh, every caress just made them yearn for each other even more! If love could be seen, touched or enacted, this was it!

Though they lay exhausted, they kissed after every few sentences. They simply could not get enough of each other.

"Karan, let's go back to the life we had," she broached the subject that was on her mind. "I can't afford to lose you again." She nuzzled her head in the crook of his arm.

"It's just what I had been thinking. I have no interest in my life if you are not a part of it. Every day, I hoped that you would change your mind and come back to me and that you would forgive me for not keeping my promise of keeping your identity hidden from the media. Little did I know that my darling was held a prisoner, alone and helpless" He felt his eyes well up again as he thought of the mental torture she must have gone through.

They lay there entwined in each other's arms, planning for a future that they had almost lost. Now, life had given them another chance, and they did not want to waste any minute of it.

The doorbell rang, and on the security camera, he could see his entire gang of friends outside the door. They both quickly got dressed, and he opened the door and asked his friends to walk inside.

All of them sat together in the room. Formal introductions were made though they all knew Fiza and she knew them. Fiza again narrated her story to them, and people were aghast as to how this could happen in the 21st century!

It was then that Karan made the announcement that he would go back to London after the peace walk to Wagah border. They were all stunned and tried to convince him not to leave something that he had started, but he had already made up his mind.

"An idea that has the power to change history is not dependent on a person or thing. It is like a wind that no one can control. It just blows and sweeps everything with it! Our idea is like that wind. We have let it loose, and soon it will create a havoc in the existing systems. For some time, it will feel like all hell has broken loose. Like a storm, it will ravage the obstacles it encounters. But when that storm subsides, beautiful peace will prevail.

The calm after the storm will make people forget their miseries and pains, and they will revel in the newly found serenity." Karan was getting carried away by his thoughts, but as he spoke, everyone was left mesmerized! Such was the power of his speech!

Every corner of the Thakur residence shone and sparkled. The best of the furnishings were out, cushions were pumped, the antique lamp was switched on, the brass items were polished till they dazzled like 100-watt bulbs, and the carpet was brushed till every hair stood out. This kind of spring cleaning had not been done in the Thakur residence for ages. This was happening today, because after years, a new would-be bride was being welcomed into the household.

The previous day, Karan had asked everyone to gather in the living room and told them about the new development. He told them the entire story of how he and Fiza had broken up, and how she had been held a prisoner by her aunt, and how she had finally managed to escape and come here. He told them that he now wanted to marry Fiza.

His father was the first one to react. While the others were still trying to absorb the news and its implications, he came over and held Karan in a tight embrace.

"Son, what I thought was an impossible and foolhardy idea, you have proven it possible. I feel proud that people today are talking about love and peace between the two countries. You have brought such a wave of love, hope and togetherness between the two countries that even politicians have started talking about re-building the relations rather than fueling animosity."

He kept his hand on Karan's shoulders as he spoke. His eyes were moist. Karan had never seen his father like this. Tears welled up in his eyes too.

"I am so proud of you, my son," he said. His entire life, Karan had wanted to hear these words from the mouth of his father. It felt like the first rain on the parched earth. His uncle and aunty also blessed him, and they all wanted to meet Fiza immediately.

So, it was decided that the next day, Fiza would come for lunch, and that was the reason why the house was undergoing a massive cleaning spree!

They did however, object to the fact that they planned to go back to London. Karan replied very firmly that he would now put her happiness before anything else in life. He had almost lost her once; he could not risk it again.

"Nothing is greater than the love I feel for my country, and I think I have done my bit. I have risked everything for the sake of peace in my country. Let others take over the baton from me. I want to live my life with the love of my life. Wherever on earth she wants to live, is where I will go with her. Apparently, she wants to live in London, and that is where I am going then."

He put across his decision very firmly. After this, no one objected, even though it was evident that they did not want him to go.

The next day, Fiza came for lunch to his house. He also invited Anu and Vivek along with Fiza. Karan's aunt kissed Fiza on her forehead and handed her a bagful of gifts. Karan's father blessed her and talked to her as if he had known her for ages!

They all had lunch, which was a vegetarian feast – *Pulao, Chana Dal, Paneer Malaidaar, Bharwaan Bhindi* in the main course and *Ras Malai* for dessert.

After the meal was over, they all discussed the future. They decided that Karan would be delivering the speech on 15th August at the Wagah border, and he would leave for London a few days after that. It was also decided to keep this news a secret so that people did not get disheartened during the march and the movement.

They planned to start the walk on the 1st of August. They would walk every day and halt at night. They would reach

Amritsar by the 13th. On 15th August, a big rally was to be organized at Wagah border on both sides.

They decided to discuss the details with the entire team in the evening. This meeting was to be held at the office, so they straightaway went there after having the meal.

The walk was not by any means a small task. The walk from Delhi to Amritsar had to have many stops, and arrangements were to be made at every stop. New people would be joining at every leg. There were many sponsors, many NGOs, many media houses, many universities and many institutions already aligned with the walk. Everything was to be coordinated. The good news was that volunteers from every walk of life were coming forward to join the movement. After years of mistrust and apathy between the two nations, they now saw a glimmer of hope, the fragrance of peace, and so, they wanted to be a part of this historic movement.

Fiza was introduced to the team without giving any further details. Only a few close people knew that she was the person who was the reason why all this had started in the first place!

Smaller teams were made and responsibilities were fixed. Everyone was very excited, and there was a nervous energy which was almost palpable.

Things were already in motion. What remained to be seen was where it would stop?

It was a lovely evening, one of those summer evenings when the sun, instead of scorching the earth in its fury, played hide-and-seek with the clouds. The clouds kept floating in the sky like wayward children who were out of control. The gentle breeze made it a perfect day to spend outdoors.

Even though the window was open and the beautiful view of the trees swaying gently in the garden was so alluring, no one had eyes for the same.

In the office of the Hindu Maha Morcha, a group of men sat in the room watching the news. The news these days was full of the 'Unite for Peace movement'. Every channel was talking about it. They were adding their own flavors to it and presenting it to the public. People were lapping it all up and asking for more. Everyone loved a good story where a knight in shining armor comes and saves people from the tyranny of evil.

So, it was being projected that the boy, Karan, was actually a knight in shining armor who had come to rescue both the countries from the politicians who were ravaging the people by plaguing them with wars and feeding them hatred.

The men in the room were worried. Things were getting out of hand. Even though they had taken steps to see that it was crushed in the beginning, they had failed. The movement, much to their dismay, had gained exponential momentum and suddenly seemed to be beyond their control.

There was one man though, who was furious and not worried. Sooraj had advocated taking harsher measures to stop him in the beginning, but the others had not agreed.

"He has become too much of a public figure," they had said, "Moreover, his father is a decorated war hero. We have to keep that in mind."

Now, things had taken an ugly shape. If Karan was allowed to continue, their party's ideological defeat was certain. They all knew this.

They had all assembled to discuss what should be done, because two days ago, the lunatics had announced the date of their march to Wagah border. They would be starting their walk on the 1st of August from Delhi, and on 15th August, they would be holding a mass rally on both sides of the border.

The movement had also gained a lot of impetus in Pakistan, though not to the extent as it had in India. The reason for its better success in India was the charismatic personality of their leader, Karan.

Sooraj had heard him a couple of times when he had gone to attend his meetings, of course in disguise, to see what he was up against. He was honestly impressed! Karan did not refer to any notes while speaking. He just spoke from his heart, and every word that he uttered, hit hard. It seemed that he was not addressing any person; he was addressing their conscience. Sooraj did not stay for long. 'If I hear him often, perhaps, he will start to change my way of thinking,' he thought wryly.

Now, more than anyone else, he knew what he was up against. He followed Karan on social media. He stalked him and was aware of his every movement. He was also aware that his girlfriend had arrived from Pakistan and that they were keeping that a secret. He had friends in their team, and he was updated on every plan, every strategy that they decided upon.

Of course, he kept all this information to himself. Right information is the key to winning even a lost battle.

The day's meeting, with only the inner circle members of the Hindu Maha Morcha, was convened to decide upon an immediate action plan to stop the march and the growing popularity of the movement.

After a lot of discussion and deliberation, Prof Tyagi looked at Sooraj and said, "We are all of the opinion that now the time has come to use harsher methods, and so we agree to let Sooraj deal with them in his own way."

Everyone nodded in agreement. There was no dissent. They dispersed, and the man who was given the big responsibility of 'fixing' the problem, sat there staring into space, lost in his thoughts.

Fiza was in seventh heaven! Her pregnancy test had come out positive! It had been nearly a month since she had come here. When she had missed her period, she had checked, and to her greatest joy, the test had been positive. Must have happened the very day she had come to Delhi, in Anu's house. In Pakistan, she had stopped taking the contraceptive, and they had not taken any precaution in the heat of the moment. She felt as if her cup would overflow with happiness!

Never in her life had Fiza known what family could be like. After meeting Karan's father, his uncle and aunties and his friends, for the first time in her life, she realized what she was missing out on.

They had not only welcomed her with open arms but had also showered her with their love. Sunidhi was such a warm person who chided her when she called her 'chachi.' "I am your Indian mother," she said. "Call me *ma* or *ammi*, whatever you feel like."

So, she decided to call her *ammi*, for she had forgotten how this word sounded on her lips. She had been 9 years old when she had last addressed someone as *ammi*.

Karan's father and uncle were also very caring and affectionate. Karan was very lucky to be born in such a loving family. Now she understood why he insisted on getting married only after taking his father's blessings. The family shared a cohesive bond of love which she found very touching. Perhaps all families were like this, or perhaps not. She was in no position to know.

When the matter of settling in London was discussed, she could see the disappointment and a lurking grief in their eyes, but they were large-hearted enough not to be obstinate about it. They did, however, try to convince him to stay in India, but when Karan said that Fiza wanted to settle in London, a neutral country, they were decent enough not to discuss it further.

Ever since the day she met his family, she had been thinking about it. She could see why his family wanted him to settle in India. India was not like what she remembered. It had made tremendous progress. The only thing that was wrong with the country was what they had set to correct. It could not be corrected by running away. What Karan had started he should take forward. The seed of love, peace and understanding that he had sown, was now a small sapling. It needed constant nurturing. He should be here to do that. Fiza understood this. Perhaps Karan also did, but he loved her too much to try to convince her to change her mind.

The day before, he had told Fiza, "I have a feeling that I do not have much time with me because I am going back. So, I have a lot of work to do. The flame that I have lighted should keep burning bright and should light up the path for the new generation. I have a lot to do."

"You can always come back from London and contribute again," she had said.

"I don't know. I somehow feel like I should do everything now. What if there is no tomorrow?" He joked.

Fiza put both her palms against her belly. It was still flat and taut. Not for long though, she smiled. A life was already there, with a tiny heartbeat, a part of her and a part of Karan, a little bit of India and a little bit of Pakistan, a symbol of their love and a symbol of unity. This was the moment when Fiza decided that she would not settle in London but in Delhi. Till the time she had not come to India and actually gotten involved in the movement, she had not understood the huge impact Karan and his movement had made on the people.

She met Ajay and Sunita, who had locked their house in their village to come to Delhi and join the movement. They were the victims of the worst kind of violent attack possible, and they had dedicated their lives to this movement for unity and peace. Fiza had heard about them but meeting them in person was truly inspiring. There were many youngsters who had left their settled life and joined the movement. In Pakistan too, Riyaz had succeeded in creating a mass movement, which was extremely commendable and motivating. Riyaz too had left behind a very promising career in London. There were no personal gains for any of them.

They were doing it for their countries, for society, for peace. So how could she be selfish?

No, they would get married in Delhi and stay here for good and work here for the betterment of society. They would raise their child here, amongst their own people. There was so much to be done. She was so excited! She felt like running to Karan and giving him the great news but he was neck-deep in the arrangements, and she did not want to disturb him at this critical juncture. So, she decided to tell him after his march to Amritsar and after his speech at the Wagah border.

He would be so happy, she thought. She could barely wait to tell him!

'It would be such a happy day when I share the news with him. Karan, you are going to be a father!' She told him for the hundredth time, albeit in her mind.

The days and the weeks passed like a jetliner that whooshes past and disappears before you can blink. The only thing that remains is a white trail that stays for a while, changes shape and slowly fades into oblivion.

All around, preparations were being made on a massive scale. The movement had caught the imagination of the people, and from all the corners of the country, help and support were pouring in. People and the media were drawing comparisons.

There had been many countrywide mass movements since the independence. Movements like the Chipko movement, Narmada Bachao and Jungle Bachao were related to saving the environment. Another movement against corruption had taken place in 2011, when an anti-corruption activist, Anna Hazare, had begun a hunger strike at the Jantar Mantar in New Delhi. It had been the beginning of a mass movement, aimed at alleviating corruption in the Indian government through the introduction of the Jan Lokpal Bill.

The movement was primarily a non-violent civil resistance, featuring demonstrations, marches, act of civil disobedience, hunger strikes, and rallies.

In 2014, the infamous Nirbhaya case—the brutal gang-rape of a young girl—had again brought together people demanding justice for the victim and security for women.

True, there were many instances of mass movements in the country but nothing had ever happened on this scale.

Earlier, the public had come together for various reasons. This time, they had come together for unity and peace. Donations were pouring in not only from within the country, but from all across the world. If two warring nations that had fought multiple wars in the past decades came together for unity and peace, it was good news for the entire world!

The executive committee expanded, and there were more experienced people who chipped in the planning and organization of the event, but the undisputed leader of the entire movement remained Karan. There were no two thoughts about it. He gave the clarion call; and the others just hoarded around him!

Different committees were formed for organizing the march from Delhi to Amritsar. Thousands of people had signed up for the march. The logistics were huge!

They decided to break the march into different legs. One leg would be covered in a day or two. They planned to halt and spend the nights in proper cities. The co-coordinator for that city was given the responsibility of making the stay arrangements for the people. Thousands of volunteers had offered to open their doors to the people who were walking in the march. Temples, gurudwaras, mosques and churches, all had come together to offer free lodging and food to the people. So, fund was not a constraint.

Karan and his team were overwhelmed by the scale of love and support they were getting from the masses. They decided to make ten stopovers where they would also be addressing the local gathering. At the other places where they had a stopover, they would only be taking a night halt. Every day, they would be walking for five to six hours before calling it a day. The rest of the day would be spent in discussions, meetings and keeping a tab on the pulse of the movement.

Peaceful demonstrations, local marches and rallies were happening in other parts of the country too, but everyone's eyes were on this march from Delhi to Wagah border and the mass rally there.

The day broke when they had to start off their walk from Delhi. It was the 1st of August 2047. The morning dawned like any other day, offering no sign or foreboding of the storm that was brewing just ahead.

They started off after a big rally at India Gate where many people addressed the gathering. School children came and sang the famous song, which was the favorite song of the father of the nation, *"Raghupati Raghav Raja Ram"*. Someone recited the Gurbani, a Christian priest uttered a prayer from the Bible and a young Muslim boy read a piece from the

Quran, invoking the blessings of Allah. The media was there to capture every moment. They wanted to talk to Karan, but there was no press conference.

"We will be talking to all of you constantly through our rallies at ten places en route," Karan told the media. "We thank you for your support in making this movement for peace and unity, a mass movement."

"What is your dream? What do you want to achieve with this march?" A reporter from the New York Times asked.

Karan smiled and closed his eyes for a moment, "My dear friend, my dream is to see a united India and Pakistan. I want to unite India and Pakistan." He opened his eyes and waved to the reporter, signaling that he wanted no more questions.

"Oh, you are the unifier! All the best, Unifier." The reporter was beaming; he had got the caption for his news story: "The Unifier Starts His March For the Union of Two Nations".

In the crowd, there was a man standing with his hands in his pockets, dark sunglasses with extra-large frames perched on his nose and a cap covering a large part of his forehead. He was standing still, deep in his thoughts, his eyes fixed on one man, the man who had just been named 'The Unifier'!

AMRITSAR

They arrived at Amritsar. It had taken them 14 days to reach the city. It had all gone as per plan till now. They had held public rallies at ten places: Sonepat, Panipat, Karnal, Kurukshetra, Ambala, Rajpura, Khanna, Ludhiana, Phagwara, and Jalandhar. The public turnout had been huge everywhere.

The stay arrangements for the group were organized at various places in Amritsar, but the main team was staying in some hostel rooms near the Golden Temple.

Karan was lying on the bed, resting his sore feet. He had lost quite a bit of weight in these two weeks. The long hours of walking under the sun had taken its toll. Even though he was physically exhausted, mentally, he was in a 'now-or-never' kind of space. He was totally charged and energized. He was ready to take on the world. This was just two countries.

Fiza was also sitting on the other side of the bed. She had just finished writing her update on the blog that she had started on the first day of the march. She named her blog, "The Unifier's March," picking the name from the news headline that had broken at the start of the march. Each day's happenings were being captured in words, images, and videos, and she was uploading them in the evenings of that same day. Even though she was travelling with the group, she did not sit on the dais of any rally. She was always in the audience.

It was at this moment that Anu entered their room.

"Hi, all set for the D-day tomorrow?" She asked Karan.

It was Fiza who replied, "His feet are hurting. I have applied some spray. We want to go to the Golden Temple and eat the *langar* there. Want to come?"

"Yes, of course!" Anu nodded in affirmation.

Fiza had read about the *Langar Sewa* at the Golden Temple and was very keen to experience it. So, they went to the temple, first had a *darshan* and then ate the *langar*.

"What did you pray for, Karan?" Anu asked on the way back to the hostel.

"I prayed that after I go back to London, this beautiful movement should not die down. This flame that we have lit should illuminate the lives of our future generation. I want my child to be born in a world where there is peace and not war, where there is love between nations and not hatred, where there are more bridges than borders." Karan was feeling very emotional today. The Golden Temple always had this effect on him. This beautiful temple, amidst the serene waters, never failed to move him.

When Karan spoke about his 'child,' instinctively, Fiza touched her belly.

Tomorrow, after the rally I will tell him, she thought.

"Karan, you can't even fathom what you have done for the nation. Without you, nothing would have been possible. I can never thank you enough," Anu said, and on an impulse hugged him.

"Everyone is turning emotional today, what's the matter?" Fiza smiled.

"Anu, I did nothing. We did everything together. We did it for no one else but for ourselves. If there is unity and peace between the countries, we will benefit," Karan replied to Anu.

It was nearly midnight when they went to sleep.

Tomorrow is the big day, Karan thought, feeling excited and exhausted at the same time. Even amidst the excitement, there was something bothering him. A feeling that he had been brushing aside for many days was now resurfacing with full force and bothering his conscience.

Yet again in his life, he was leaving something incomplete! Yet again, he was giving up something before taking it to its logical conclusion! For the first time in his life, his father was proud of him. His son had set out to achieve something and had not given up mid-way. In fact, for the first time in his life, Karan was proud of himself, but like always, this time too, he was leaving his work incomplete. He was abandoning an idea which was his baby. Leaving it like an orphan. He was choosing the self before the nation. When did he become so selfish? He had noticed the pain in his father's eyes when he had mentioned about going back to London. No, he could not do this! He could not let his father down again!

Moreover, if he abandoned the movement now, Anu would certainly get aligned with Ekta Party and the entire sanctity of it being a mass movement would be lost! That would be so detrimental to the cause! No, he could not allow this to happen! He would have to talk to Fiza about it. However much he loved her, one thing he knew now for sure — the nation and humanity should come before the self. He would stay here and work for the nation. After the rally tomorrow, I will tell her, he thought.

Destiny, somewhere, was weaving an intricate pattern which no one would be able to decipher. What we don't understand, we accept. That is why we accept what destiny unfolds to us. Sometimes, we like to fool ourselves into believing that we can create our own destinies. That is when destiny has the last laugh.

WAGAH BORDER

The march had come to its final destination, the Wagah border. There were thousands of people who had come for this final leg of the march. Karan's family had also flown from Delhi, and they were sitting in the front row in the audience.

On the dais were Karan, Anu, Vivek, Manpreet and Iqbal. Everyone spoke for a few minutes. Now, it was Karan's turn to speak. People had come from far-off places to listen to his speech.

He held the microphone and walked to the dais to address the crowd. The crowd started cheering him even before he began his speech. The moment that he started to speak, everyone fell quiet.

"'At the stroke of midnight, when the world sleeps, India will wake up to life and freedom.' Exactly a hundred years ago, our first Prime Minister, Pandit Jawahar Lal Nehru, had uttered these words. These words were like a breath of fresh air to the people who were being choked to death by the oppression and tyranny of the colonial masters. These words had given them a new lease of life, a ray of hope, a sliver of light in the dark of the night.

"India was finally free! Of course, this freedom had come at a heavy price — a very heavy price! In the joyous moment, we decided not to concentrate on the cost of freedom, but to savor every moment of its new acquirement. Sometimes, a simple mistake can cost you the very thing that you are trying to preserve. This mistake by our forefathers has cost us our very soul. The freedom was gained by sacrificing the very essence of our country — unity in diversity.

"We chose to divide ourselves into two.

"I know, a hundred years later, we cannot and should not pass judgment on their decision for we can't really understand in totality what their compulsions were and what the options then were. But one thing we do know is that things did not stop at the division of our country. Our masters were very shrewd; as if dividing the country was not enough, they left an open wound, a wound that would continue to hurt. They created a never-ending chasm between the two nations. And like fools, we, instead of building bridges, continued to fight over borders, and thereby, we let our colonial rulers succeed in their devious plans!

"Once in a while, there have been people across both sides of the border, who have shouted at the top of their voices saying, 'Look, don't get caught in the trap that they have laid for us. It's not late yet. Let's not talk of hatred; let's talk of peace. It's never too late for peace!' But alas! People with vested interests, the warmongers, the hate mongers, always crushed their voices. They were silenced with force. Every time, hate won and love lost.

"Not anymore. This time, the voices are not one or two, but many. This time, the youths from either side have united. We don't want war, we want peace. We want to unite. Why? We all know the reason. But how and when, needs to be worked out.

"We are not saying that it will happen overnight. An idea that has the power to change the future of humankind will not manifest into a reality in a day, a month or even a year. It might take many years; maybe another hundred years for it to turn into a reality.

"It is possible that it might never happen. But can we at least make a beginning? Can we not at least try? Not as a person or a political party but as citizens of two independent countries. Try to bridge the gap that was forced upon us. Try to heal the hearts that have been bleeding for a hundred years. Try to talk of love and peace, not of hate and war.

"Today, after the world has seen the mass destruction of two world wars, the threat of the third world war is looming large over us, and with many countries being nuclear powers, the nuclear bomb is ticking under us...tick tock tick tock.

"It can go off any moment, destroying not one or two nations, but the whole of mankind!

"So, we all agree that the greatest evil today is the nuclear bomb. But I beg to differ. The greatest evil is not the nuclear bomb, but it is the hate. It is the hate that resides in the minds of people of one nation against people of another nation or caste or creed or religion.

"A hundred years ago, we had patriots. Today, we have nationalists. There is a huge difference! Patriotism is to love your country along with its diversity, all its castes, creeds and religions, whereas nationalism talks about the supremacy of a nation over another. My father is a patriot. He was wounded and lost an eye and an arm in the war. In his battalion, he had Muslims, Christians and Sikhs, who fought for the nation as ONE!

"He is a true patriot. And today, many people in the country are calling his son a traitor. Why? Because he is talking about unity; he is talking about peace.

"I don't care if talking about unity and peace with Pakistan makes me a traitor. I would rather be a traitor and unite the two nations than be a nationalist and divide them.

"I don't care if I am thrown in prison for this. I am the voice of the conscience of common people across both sides of the border. At this very moment, across the border, in Pakistan, my friend is singing the same tune — the melody of peace.

"Powerful people who thrive on wars like the devil thrives on blood, are having restless nights, I am told. They are trying to find ways and means to crush this demand for a new dawn.

"But tell me, after a dark night, can dawn be far away? Can you stop the dawn from breaking?

"You can kill one Karan, but there are hundreds on both sides of the border.

"You can kill me today..."

As if someone had been waiting for his permission to shoot, a single bullet was fired with the precision of a surgeon, aimed straight at his heart.

No one could understand what was happening, as one moment he was speaking and in the next, he was on the ground.

People thought that he had collapsed. It was Anu who first noticed his white shirt turning red.

"He has been shot!" She screamed and rushed towards the motionless body lying on the ground. "Please, please help! Ambulance!" She was shouting.

She cradled the unconscious figure in her arms, sobbing unashamedly.

The microphone on his lapel, which was still functioning, was now amplifying her sobs, and it was now clear to everyone that something untoward had happened.

Vivek gently took Karan's motionless figure in his arms and, with the help of others, rushed towards the ambulance which had been parked as a safety measure.

It was no mean task to carry that lifeless body to the ambulance, as Vivek had to cut through the crowd to reach there.

Someone took over the other microphone and was giving instructions to the crowd to stay calm and disperse without creating any ruckus.

The crowd, which had been spellbound listening to Karan's charismatic voice, was now bewildered to see him being carried away in the arms of his friend.

Vivek knew that even if he managed to fly to the ambulance or the hospital, it would be of no use. The bullet had found its mark. He was not carrying his friend. He was carrying his lifeless body.

Everything happened in a whirlwind after Karan was murdered in broad daylight, in the middle of giving a speech about love, peace and tolerance.

One moment, Fiza was listening to Karan's power-packed speech, feeling proud of him as she caressed her belly that was carrying the fruit of their love, and in the next moment, there was the sound of a shot and everything went haywire. A mayhem ensued, during which Fiza vaguely remembered seeing Vivek carry Karan in his arm, shouting for an ambulance. There was blood! Oh My God, Karan! Her Karan had been shot! Fiza did not remember what happened next as she lost her consciousness.

When she woke up, she was in a hospital, with many people around her. It was Karan's aunt who hugged her tight and sobbed into her ears.

"He is gone, Fiza. Our Karan is gone. They killed him. When they could not silence his voice, they silenced him." She was wailing now.

Fiza could not breathe. She could not feel anything. Is Karan dead? There must be a mistake. She must be dreaming. She always had nightmares where she would live through her fears, but when the nightmare became unbearable, she used to wake up. She would wake up soon, she told herself.

It was then that Karan's lifeless body was wheeled inside the room, and the cot was placed next to hers. So, it was not a nightmare after all. Karan was dead. No, she was dead before she had even started living. She felt an anger so fierce that it felt like someone had put a dagger in her heart. This could not happen to her. No one could be so cruel to do this to her.

"No!" She screamed and passed out again.

NEW DELHI

The days that followed passed like a mist. She would wake up and pass out again. Her conscious mind was refusing to accept the fact that Karan was gone, and it preferred to take comfort in nothingness. She remembered seeing Riyaz, who had come from Pakistan. Jawed *bhai jaan* had also come for the funeral and wanted to take her back.

Go back? Where? She had no family to go back to. Karan had been her family, and now his family was her family too. London seemed eons away. She had no life there too.

Her Karan was here. His ashes were immersed in the Ganges. His family was here. His soul was here. She could not go anywhere and leave him behind. Karan's child would not grow up without knowing his family. She would stay here.

The thing Karan cared the most for, his idea, should not die with him. She would take it forward. Yes, once she gained some strength, she would start working for his dream of love, peace and union. Karan's baby in her womb gave her a reason to live, and the decision to work for Karan's idea gave her future life a purpose.

Even in the darkness of the grief, the news that Fiza was pregnant brought a smile back to the faces of his family members. They heaved a sigh of relief when they came to know that Fiza was not going back. They had fervently hoped that she would stay. Even though the son of the family had gone, they were looking forward to their grandchild.

After years, a baby would come into the household, and he, perhaps, would fill the void that Karan's death had left. Hope flickered like a tiny star, very far away but nonetheless bringing some light in their lives and giving them the strength to pull through.

It's not the air that we breathe that keeps us alive; it is the hope and purpose. Karan's family found a hope to cling on to, and Fiza found a purpose to live for.

Together, they decided to give life another chance.

Anu was sitting in her office in New Delhi. Her back ached from sitting at her work desk for hours. It was a never-ending work, and she was exhausted. The last month had gone like a whirlwind.

The person who had fired the bullet could not be caught as he had disappeared in the crowd. Even though he fled, everyone was talking openly that the murder had been planned by the HMM group. They could see that Karan was becoming a threat to all that they stood for. Even the media was blatantly blaming them for this cowardly act, and the police also faced a lot of flak for not being able to arrest the culprit. There were mass protests outside HMM's offices across the country, and effigies of Prof Tyagi were burned at many places.

After Karan was killed, the mass support that was already continuously pouring in turned into a hysteria. There were calls from all quarters to form a political party and start working for the cause. Even Karan's father had called her up and told her that even though Karan was against integrating politics with the cause, it made sense to form a political party and fight for the cause from inside.

"Beta, you should carry on the fight that Karan started. I have no doubt that today's youth has the power to do anything, but to change the system, you have to be in the system. Sitting outside, you cannot make much of a difference. People will support you for some time, and then they will get busy with some other cause. So, make a political party and keep working for the cause," said the broken man, a man who had not broken down even when the enemies had tortured him for months, but had sobbed like a child when he lit the pyre of his only son.

They launched a political party and named it 'The Unifier.' They planned to contest the elections and started preparing.

The media had been very supportive throughout the campaign, and even after the party was formed, they were getting largely positive coverage. The entire electoral tide seemed to be in their favor. Anu, being the president of the party, knew that she would soon be a part of the Indian political circle.

Vivek, Sudha, Sumit, Manpreet, Iqbal, Ajay and Sunita were all members of the executive committee.

There was a beep on Anu's phone. She looked at it and frowned. 'Why does Sooraj want to meet me?'

She had made it very clear that she did not want anything to do with him. On impulse, she picked it up on the first ring.

"Congratulations on your new party!" He said.

"Why are you calling me?" Anu did not bother with the niceties.

"I want to meet you alone," he replied.

"Neither am I interested, nor do I have the time," she said with abhorrence.

"I am telling you that you are better off hearing what I have to say in private. So, it's in your interest that you meet me," he suddenly sounded very stern.

"Okay. When and where?"

"At our usual café, right now. I am waiting for you. Be there in ten minutes," he said and disconnected the call.

Anu looked at the pile of work on her table and sighed. This man had a great nuisance value and could not be ignored. A lot was at stake now. So, she took her car keys from the table and went out to meet him.

He was already there when she reached, sitting at 'their' table and sipping a beer. He had already ordered her favorite drink, she noticed.

"So, you got what you wanted," he said, looking straight into her eyes.

"Yes, so what? What's your problem? Let's fight the election. We are going to wipe off your party not only from Delhi, but from the political scene of the whole country," she said with a smirk.

"You loved that guy!" Sooraj did not ask but made a statement.

For a moment, Anu was quiet. Her face softened as she remembered Karan.

"Yes, so what?" She replied again.

"Anu, no one knows you better than me. But even I fail to understand, and I am curious to know. Why did you get him killed?"

Anu's face went ashen as if all the blood had been sucked out of her body.

"What the hell are you saying? Have you gone mad?" She barely managed to whisper and tried to leave.

"Not so fast. We have a lot to talk about." Sooraj caught hold of her hand and pulled her back onto the chair.

"There is no need to pretend. I know. After you tried to kill Sakshi when you came to know that I loved her, I did not press any charges against you because I cared for you too. I knew that you were not mentally stable at that time. That was my mistake. I should have handed you over to the police then itself."

Anu kept quiet with a deadpan face.

"I always knew you were ambitious. So, when I saw the entire drama unfold before me and you still did not try to form any political party, I knew something was wrong. I kept an eye on you. In fact, to be honest, I have always kept an eye on you. I knew when you contacted the mercenary.

"I thought you were planning to kill Fiza, for I knew that you were in love with Karan. It was only at the last moment that it struck me that the victim was not Fiza, but Karan himself. His death would open up the gates for you. You knew that he would never marry you even if Fiza was killed. You also knew that if he were alive, he would never agree to form a political party. After his death, not only could you make one, but also get the sympathy votes and perhaps even win the election!

"The moment I realized this, I sent a message to Karan, but he did not pay any heed. I rushed to the venue, but it was too late. I could not save Karan but managed to nab the paid mercenary. The police could not find him, because he is still my captive.

"I was thinking of going to the police, but I thought of coming and meeting you before that. So, what do you have to say to all this?"

Anu, by now, was slightly composed. Her eyes had a glazed look, but there were moments when the mask fell off and the hatred shone through them.

"Sooraj, if you know me, then I know you equally well. If I am ambitious, so are you. I always used to say that we were like two peas in a pod, so very similar. We could have had a good life together. Together, we could have become very powerful. Power was what both of us had wanted then. Power is what both of us want, even today. Only, the ways we chose to attain power were different.

"If I am a murderer, so are you. If I killed Karan, you too killed him by not stopping the murder."

Sooraj laughed at this, throwing back his head.

"Don't laugh. I am in no mood for jokes. It suited you to let Karan die. Alive, he was of no use to you. You never messaged Karan. His phone was with me when he was speaking.

"What good is he to me dead?" Sooraj asked, leaning towards Anu.

"If he was not, you would not be here talking to me, but you would have been at the police station. I know why you are here, and I am happy that you are here. I always said that we make a good pair, didn't I? HMM has been totally washed out. It might take years for it to be revive and come to power. On the contrary, we will come to power soon; if not in this election, surely in the next. Everyone knows this. Even you. Let's wait for the right time, and you can join us. You care for the Hindus no more than I care for peace! We both care for power and money. I am about to get the sun in my hands. You could have stopped me, but you did not, for you also wanted some sunshine, didn't you?"

Sooraj smiled. Anu was right. They were both like two peas of the same pod. Very sharp, intelligent, greedy and ruthless!

Even though the fact that Sooraj knew about her scheme came as a shock to her, she did not take much time to get over her shock and catch on to his motive. She sure was shrewd!

Anu's brain was now working at rocket-speed to analyze how this new development might hamper her plans. She had not worked so hard, and planned so meticulously to lose it all. Fiza not going back to Pakistan also worked in her favor. People sympathized with her, and this would surely get her more votes. Fiza never guessed that she had leaked her name to the media. She had hoped that Fiza would succumb to her aunt's pressure and give up on Karan. That had almost happened, but Karan made it clear that he considered Anu only as a friend and nothing more.

Nothing was really lost. She would have to involve Sooraj in her plans. It was better. She could use him to garner support from some of the hardliners too. Moreover, it gets lonely at the top. You need someone who can understand you, someone who is like you. They would never trust each other, but they would never betray each other either.

'Yes, I can use him,' she thought.

Dusk was falling and darkness was creeping in. With dawn would come a new tomorrow. The light would cut through the darkness and everything would be bright again. But there was no light which could dispel the darkness that had permeated the souls of the two people sitting in the dark corner of that popular Delhi café.

15TH AUGUST 2057
NEW DELHI

"Mom! Get dressed quickly. We don't want to be late for the flag hoisting ceremony at the Red Fort," Krish implored his mother. He was very excited. His beloved aunt, Anu, who was the Home Minister of the country, had arranged for passes for them to watch the flag hoisting from the VIP stand.

Fiza stopped whatever she was doing and looked at the animated face of her son, Krish, whose full name was Krishan Thakur Khan. He was all of nine and bubbling with life. He was the exact replica of his father, even at this young age. Even after all these years, Fiza felt an emptiness in her heart and in her life whenever she thought of Karan. Some vacuums can never be filled. He had left the world for a place where, she hoped, there were no borders or war, only love and peace. Before leaving, he had given people a valuable gift though — a gift of hope!

He had given them hope — hope to dream, hope to strive for unity and hope to believe that nothing was impossible.

The Unifier Party, whose seeds he had sown with his own hands, had grown from strength to strength, and today, Anu was the Home Minister. There were a lot of expectations from her. The public wanted her to weave miracles. Karan had brought the country's masses together for a common cause; now they wanted Anu to fulfil those promises. They expected things to change.

Not Fiza! The past ten years had taught her many lessons. Not long after Karan was killed, Sooraj joined the party. It came as a shock for many, but Anu managed to convince everyone that he had changed. He rose up the party ranks and soon became a center of power. Fiza could never understand how a person could have a complete 360-degree change of heart. He now looked after the defence portfolio.

The union that Karan dreamed of did not happen but there were new beginnings. There were some trade openings between the two countries. Travel had become easier, and there were collaborations in some areas of businesses. Apparently, it looked as if efforts were being made to bring about peace and cooperation.

That was on the surface! However, things had not changed much. Every day, there was news of firings across the LOC. The countries were busy hoarding weapons to protect their borders. There was not much real progress even after years of Karan laying down his life for the cause.

The common public across both sides of the border still wanted peace and unity. But alas, the sacrifice of one Karan was not enough. It needed many more sacrifices before it could become a reality, if ever!

Some things don't change. People might want a change, but politics doesn't change. Does power corrupt you? We don't really know, but it sure does change the outlook. Fiza had come to this conclusion in the last ten years. At times, she felt that Anu had become like any other politician, worried only about power, not nourishing the idea that was sown by Karan.

But even then, Fiza was quite happy. She was happy because Karan had left her a gift — the gift of hope!

She still dreamt of a day when there would be no borders between countries. No boundaries! Freedom to live and love beyond boundaries! She was still working for it. She, in Delhi, and Riyaz, in Islamabad, were working continuously to fulfill the dream that Karan has seen.

Was it possible? Perhaps not, and certainly not in their lifetime! But one could certainly hope for it, and that was what kept her going.

What would a life bereft of hope be like?

The unifier that unites nations cannot come from politics. It should be in the hearts of people. Love can be the only unifier.

Love should unite humankind, irrespective of caste, country or religion.

'Let my son wake up in that borderless world one day,' Fiza said a mental prayer. She hugged her son and said, "Come on, let's go. Let's dream some more and hope some more."

ABOUT THE AUTHOR

Rashmi Trivedi is an author, poet and an explorer, working at a middle Management level in a leading PSU. She entered the literary world in May 2016 with her first book, Woman, Everything Will Be Fine, which became a bestseller in its genre. She then came out with her poetry collection titled Handful of Sunshine, Pocketful of Rain, in December 2017. Many of her poems went viral on the social media.

Her subsequent novel, From Ashes to Dreams, published in August 2018, climbed to the no.2 spot on the Amazon hot-seller list within a few days, and went on to sell more than 15,000 copies.

Renowned for putting forward remarkable ideas through her publications, the bestselling author has now taken her biggest stride in the literary field with her first futuristic fiction, 2047: The Unifier.

A working mother of two children, Trivedi feels life has been a great teacher, and reveals that she is always in love—with life! She lives in New Delhi, India.

To know more about her visit
rashmitrivedi.com
Write to her at:
contact@rashmitrivedi.com

THE END